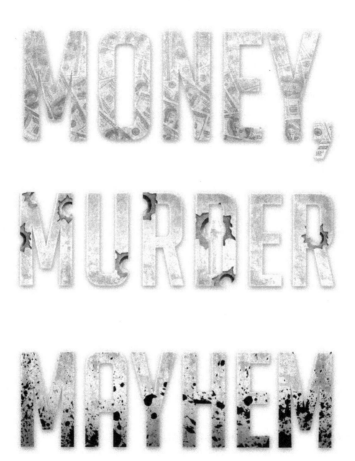

Sean Branch/www.SeanLBranch.com

Publishing Concierge: The TariqSphere
Washington, DC/20019
Cover Design/Interior Design by: The TariqSphere | www.thetariqsphere.com

First Trade Printing: August 2018

Money, Murder & Mayhem -- 1st ed.

ISBN : 978-0-9964330-4-4

DISCLAIMER

This novel is a work of fictional tales from the author's imagination. The contents within this book are not meant to glorify or influence any specific violent behavior. Any references, resemblance or similarities of actual events, real people living or dead and any real locales are intended to give the novel a sense of reality. Any similarities in other names, characters, places and incidents of true events in real life are entirely coincidental.

DEDICATION

This book is dedicated to the men and women that fell victim to the streets who are no longer with us, and also the men and women we lost to the system who continue to remain firm against the oppressions of the system. Who never wavered in their principles, and who remained honorable throughout it all. Keep your heads up, remain strong and stay vigilant in your fight to reclaim your freedom. I respect you all and salute you to the highest degree.-SB

ACKNOWLEDGEMENTS

First and foremost I want to give thanks and praise to the Most Gracious and Most Merciful Allah (SWA) for keeping me mentally strong with the understanding and the intellect to deal with life's adversities head on.

To my loving and supportive family who had my back through it all despite my faults. To my beautiful daughter Diamond who's always been my reason for giving a fuck. To my heart Nesia: You're my Mary to my Method. You're all I need to get by. To my son, my prince Sean Branch Jr. Rest in Peace my man. You may be gone, but never forgotten. My rock, the queen of the Branch Family; my beautiful grandmother. You're truly missed. May you rest in eternal peace. Till we meet again.

To my Pops; "Descansa en paz padre Te Amo"

To the strongest lady I know; my beautiful sometimes crazy mother. I love you for never believing the lies the government said about me, and for being there for me and never giving up on me despite all that I took you through as a young hard-headed kid. To my aunts Leora, Arnita, Maureen (R.I.P), Tandra. My uncles Aaron, Spud-neck Wade, Boney Clyde, Big Jerry (R.I.P), My cousins Brother Love (R.I.P), Jerry(R.I.P.)

My cousins, Tanona, Rob, Nicole, Shauntia, Nee-Cee, Jamari, Prudence

SEAN BRANCH

To my extended family "The Holloman's" Momma Holloman, Neal, Toni, Trayon, My brother Gee (R.I.P.), Rell (R.I.P.), Jeff, Doc, Donnell. The Floyd family, Doris, Hazel, James, Curtis, Jr. (R.I.P)

To my angel Ms. Betty and my brother Go-Go.

Mustafa and Yvette Tariq for believing in me enough to take a chance on me. Words can never express how much I truly appreciate you both.

My man Eyone. What's understood; needs no explanation. Jason Poole, Anthony "Bucky" Fields, NeNe Capri for lacing me with the knowledge to jump start my first novel.

Fry, Ishmeal Ford-Bey, Jo-Jo Greene, Titus, La-La, Bam, Mario, Larry Moe, Dom, Kevin "Fatt Daddy" Jackson, Trey, Opio, Big Mark Ford, Jerry, Big Melvin, Big Lo, Head, Bush Whack, Tone, Angelo "Nut" Daniels, Baby Face Ronzell, Nhemiah, R. st. Mack, Black, Dre, Kevin Grey, Kobi & Karim 100 films.

Lil Stink, Lil Marvin, Jamal, Nu-Nu, T-Bone, G-5, Zeek, Big E, Lil Boogie, Black Lover, Oldest Boi DJ, JV, Adolf, Spock Ears, Antonio Jones, Duck Sauce, Kid, Egg Yoke, R.E. Moe Man, Keith Holmes, Chico, Mike Greg, cCc Mike, cCc Bee, Boobie, Big Mike, Sharron, Doug, Baggs, Kent,Monkey D, Don, Black,Congo Ray, Big Andy, J.B. Pippy, Rusty, Pork, I.vi, Butt-Butt, My sister Pig, Kaos, Hunka, Taco, Bo, Junior, Dice Head, Mood, Pat, FatNate, Dave Battle, Young Chris, East Gate Fatts, Fox, Smiley, BBD, Scrap, Rafiq, Raf, Rico, Bird, Malik (Bouncy), 10th Ward Fatts, 2 Gun Salute C.B., Baby Hec, Mack 11,

Ju-Ju, Lean, Preach, J-Rock, N.Y. Lou, Domincio (R.I.P.), B-More Bun-Rod, Beanie, Coach Umar & Jameelah, Furqaan "The Embroidery Store", 18th & D twins Derrick & Darryl Moore, Black Jesus Tay, K-May, PeeWee, Rome, Brick House (R.I.P.) Tony & Dickie Morgan, Ms. Cookie Mayo, Danielle, Lynn, K.C., Shawn Lee, Barber Shop Norman.

CONTENTS

CHAPTER ONE

THE BEGINNING

"It is said that a child's mind is like a sponge. They learn quickly what they see. Early teachers make the most powerful impact." –SB

The year was 1982, Ronald Reagan was the 40th President of the United States of America. Powder cocaine was the drug of choice amongst the middle class throughout the Nation's Capital. Everyone from your next door neighbor, school teachers, doctors, prominent attorneys, judges, athletes, entertainers – all the way up to members of Congress on Capitol Hill, all got high on what they called… "Nose Candy."

Dontay was the tender age of 11 years young when cocaine was flowing rapidly through the city streets of Washington D.C. He was a smart kid, very charismatic for his age. He expressed an extremely unique gift of persuasion, and often times used that gift to get himself out of trouble. His friends, Dan, Pat, and Calvin would joke around and call him Sanchez because of his hazel eyes and curly hair; they would associate his looks to the reason why he always got his way. His mother was a Hecht's company warehouse employee by day and an Avon cosmetics hustler by night. She would grind long hours going door to door selling her beauty products to make a few extra coins to pursue her real passion in real estate.

She truly took pride in her grind. So, when she had to take off from her day job because Dontay had gotten into a fight at school with a classmate name Marquise, she was furious and was ready to give him the ass whipping of his young life. An ass whipping that he would remember up until he was 40. Forcing her to have to clock out 5 hours before her quitting time, and especially with Dontay knowing she didn't play about having to take off work for nonsense. She arrived at the school in 10 minutes and approached the Principal's office. Just before stepping inside, she held on to the door knob and listened to her 11 year old talk his way out of a suspension.

"How are we supposed to receive an education if we're suspended?" Dontay asked the Principal. "I'm sorry for what I did, and I promise it will never happen again! What we did was wrong and we both take responsibility for our actions, so can you please just give us some extra chores after school instead of a suspension...because a mind is a terrible thing to waste?!"Principal Mercer chuckled at the young man's charisma.

"We can sweep the floors, empty the trash, and clean the chalk boards, but please don't suspend us. We really need to be in school learning."

Standing outside of the door, she couldn't believe her ears, but smiled when she overheard the Principal agree to Dontay's form of punishment, and at that very moment; she realized that he had a gift.

Not getting suspended saved him from getting his ass tore out the frame, but she was still upset for losing those 5 hours at work, and had to make up that money. So, as a punishment, no basketball at the local recreation center, no football, no riding his bike and no ripping and running up and down the streets with his friends. She made him tag along with her every evening for a week while she went door to door throughout the entire neighborhood selling her Avon cosmetic products.

After 3 days of doors not being answered or people flat out saying NO and slamming the door in their faces as if they were Jehovah witnesses, Dontay could no longer stand the look of hurt and embarrassment in his mother's eyes. The next door his mother knocked on, a heavy set woman with a short afro answered and before his mother could get a word out, Dontay took charge and blurted out "She's pretty ain't she Ma?" He said with a smile on his face from ear to ear. "Why thank you young man, you're a handsome little thing yourself." The heavy set lady said as she gently pinched his cheek. "She'll probably like that peach bubble gum lipstick you sold the other lady!" He said as he looked up at his mother who was temporarily puzzled as to what he was talking about because she hadn't sold anyone anything all evening. But, she quickly caught on. "Peach Bubble Gum Lipstick?" the woman curiously asked. "Oh yeah! It's very good, and your husband will love how it tastes when you kiss him!" Dontay said as both women burst out with laughter. "What do you know about kissing?" The heavy set woman asked jokingly with a light chuckle in her voice. "In that case, give me two of them. And two strawberry and one of those scented candles, and the body wash too."

Dontay spit the exact same game on the next four houses and got them to spend $40 each. "Boy, you're a natural! I need to bring you with me more often." She said with a smile, as the money piled up in her purse.

Once they got home, she counted the $238 she made thanks to her son. She noticed how every female customer relished at how cute her son was, and how quickly they would go get their purse soon after. After a long evening of walking, he took a hot bath, and then got in bed. His mother entered into his bedroom and sat on the edge of his bed. "Thank you son! You really helped your mamma out tonight. I was ready to throw in the towel and call it quits when that lady slammed the door in my face, but you stepped in and saved the day. "My little Prince" she said with a smile and rubbed his leg.

"I've noticed something about you this week. Something that I never paid attention to before, until now. God blessed you with a talent of persuasion. Some people may call it the gift of gab, but how you choose to use that talent is up to you." She kissed him on the cheek, got up and made her exit from his room. Turned around at the door, blew him a kiss, then turned off the lights and shut the door.

CHAPTER

TWO

OFF THE PORCH

"Be it true or false, what is said about men often has as much influence upon their lives and especially upon their destinies, as what they do." –Victor Hugo

---

The next morning he got up and went to school. While walking down the hall with his friend Calvin, he noticed a dude named Marquise approaching him with a mean look on his face. Not knowing his intentions, he stopped and balled his fist up as tight as he could and prepared himself for battle.

"What's up Calvin?" Marquise said, and then turned his attention towards Dontay. They stared at each other for minute, then Marquise extended his hand as to indicate that he came in peace and didn't want any trouble. Dontay was reluctant to oblige, but after a moment's hesitation and carefully surveying Marquise's demeanor and eye contact; he accepted Marquise's hand shake as a form of peace. At that moment, a friendship between the two was formed. "Thanks for speaking up for me yesterday with Principal Mercer. My mother would've killed me if I got suspended".

"Don't mention it!"

"You wanna go the carry-out at lunch time? My treat!" Marquise said as he held up the biggest bank roll Dontay ever seen in his life. "DAMN! Where you get all that money from? You robbed somebody or something?" He naively asked?

Marquise burst out laughing, and put the money back in his pocket. "Naw, I ain't rob nobody." He looked over his shoulder from side to side to make sure no one was in earshot to hear him, leaned forward and proudly said... "I be hustling!" Giving Dontay a devilish grin, then turned on his heels and began walking down the hall.

"Hustling???" Dontay naively asked as he ran up alongside of Marquise, leaving AL standing alone at his locker. "Shhhhh! Man, don't say that out loud. The wrong person might hear you, but yeah, I be hustling up Montana. You wanna go see what it's like after school?"

Intrigued by all the money Marquise had in his pocket, he didn't think twice and jumped out there head first with no consideration of the consequences he'd face if his mother found out he hooked school and went to one of the most notorious and drug infested neighborhoods in the city. A pestilent neighborhood that she warned him several times to stay away from...a warning that he took heed to until now.

He couldn't believe his eyes when he stepped foot onto Montana Terrace Housing Projects.

He felt like he just stepped into another world. A world that he was not yet exposed to, until he met Marquise.

The atmosphere was thumpin' and everyone was moving too fast for him to keep up. Hand to hand sells were going on all around him from boys and girls as young as 12 years old, up to men and woman as old as 50 years his senior. It was the norm, a way of life, and a means of survival.

"What's up youngin?" Someone said from behind him, breaking his concentration. The voice of the man responsible for the bankroll in Marquise's pockets. The man who could easily make or break you in the hustling business, especially on Montana Terrace.

"Who Dis?" He asked. Looking Dontay up and down with a menacing stare as he counted his money. "Dis my man Dontay."

"What you doing up here shorty?" He asked, not once taking his eyes off his money as he continued to count it. One thing his father told him was to never respect a man that couldn't look you in the eye while he's talking to you.

"He wanna hustle." Marquise blurted out before Dontay could even fix his lips to answer. That wasn't what he wanted because he didn't have a clue what hustling was or what he was about to get himself involved in. What he did know was that he wanted some of that money Marquise had in his pocket, and what the man known as Kool was now counting in his face, and without a second thought; he took a leap of faith into a life of uncertainty.

"Yeah, I wanna hustle."He said...and at that very moment, he entered a world that would change his life forever.

Kool smiled, then put his arm around Dontay's frail shoulders, and walked him over to the side of the recreation center where a small group of young boys around his age were shooting dice. They approached a kid who looked like he couldn't have been any more than 10 years old sitting on a milk crate. Kool held up his hand to motion the young runner to bring him the package.

"Here, hold dis." He said and handed him 5 small zip lock baggies with white powder inside.

"You know what that is?" Kool asked. Dontay looked at the baggies in his hand, then looked at

Kool... "Nah! What is it?"

"That right there is cocaine and also a 10 year prison sentence. First things first, if you get in this game, you gotta keep your mouth shut about my business, you understand? What I mean by that is, if you ever get caught by the police, you didn't get that from me. The most important rule to this game and your survival out here is you never snitch, you understand?"

Dontay shook his head yeah in the affirmative.

"You think you ready for this?" Dontay licked his chapped lips and rubbed his hands together in excitement, and said yeah.

"Aiight dig dis. Those baggies are halves, they go for $50 a bag. You give me $35 off each bag and you keep $15 for yourself. Don't hold them on you. Stash 'em where only you know where they are. Niggaz is grimy up here, if they know where your shit is at, it's gone. After every sell, give Marquise the $35. One more thing, if the jump-outs ever snatch you up, you don't know anything understand?"

"Yeah, I understand! Never tell." Dontay said.

Kool gave him a slight grin. "Aiight, get to work. I'll see you later." Kool turned on his heels and stepped off towards the building. He motioned Marquise with a head nod in Dontay's direction.

"It's time to go to work baby, you ready?" Marquise asked rubbing his hands together.

"Yeah but, who am I supposed to give this to?"

"Don't worry about all that, I got you. Just stand right here and I'mma bring you the customers. All you gotta do is give 'em what they ask for and get the money. Stash the bag right there in the bushes, I'll be right back."

Ten minutes went by...which to Dontay, seemed like a lifetime. Marquise approached him with a tall old looking guy who had a bad case of the twitch.

"He want 2 for $90." Marquise said. Dontay reached in the bushes and gave him 2 bags. The old man with the twitch opened the bag, stuck his finger inside and tasted the powder. He gave them a head nod of approval, handed him the cash, and bent the corner before they even realized he was gone.

"Here you go." Dontay handed Marquise the $90 and Marquise peeled off the $20 and handed it back to Dontay.

"How it feel?"

"How what feel?"

"How does it feel to officially be in the game with your first sell? You're a hustler now baby."

Marquise said, as he tapped Dontay on his shoulder with a smile like a proud big brother.

After his very first drug sell, he stood there looking in amazement at the $20 in his hand, then looked around at the older guys twice his age making sell after sell and collecting money. Thoughts flooded his mind, and he couldn't believe he was standing smack dab in the middle of Montana Terrace selling drugs with grown men twice his age. He quickly caught on and wanted to make more money. He was a bit caught off guard by the money bug, but could hear his mother's voice in his head...**"Stay your ass from off that hill and away from that project!**"His thoughts were interrupted by a tap on his shoulder that almost made his soul jump out of his little body.

"Damn man! You scared the shit out of me."

"What you doing up here shorty?"

"I must be sticking out like a sore thumb or something." He said. And after making his first drug sell, he felt confident enough to answer "I'm hustling, I'm a hustler!" Rocko laughed.

"Who your little ass up here hustling for?"

"I can't tell you that."

"Yeah OK, I respect that. But, I already saw Kool hollering at you. When you ready to be a real hustler and make some real money, holla at me." Rocko turned and walked away. Rocko was 17 years old, another established hustler who had his own crew. He was his own boss that ran a crew of young hustlers that all dressed in velour Fila sweatsuits, and wore big gold rope necklaces. Rocko drove a champagne gold XJ5 Jaguar, and his team of youngins' all had scooters.

Rocko gave a package to whoever wanted to get money. He gave the have-nots a way to have knots in their pockets. The allure of how Rocko and his team shined was enticing to Dontay's young eyes. They looked like they were winning, and he wanted to be on the winning team. While he stared and admired Rocko and his crew, a deep voice broke his concentration once again...

"Shorty, Aye Shorty!"

"What's up Twitch man? I mean big man!"

"You still working?" Twitch asked, rubbing his hands together then rubbed his dirty hands across his face.

"Yeah, what you need?"

"Give me the same thing 2 for $90." They made the transaction and Twitch bent the corner and disappeared. Dontay looked at the corner of the building to see where Twitch had gone, but he was nowhere in sight, nor was Marquise. He was starting to feel out of place like a goldfish in water filled with piranhas. An hour had gone by and Marquise was still M.I.A.

"Jump Outs! Jump Outs!" Someone yelled, and before he even knew what was happening around him, people started running in a frantic frenzy. He didn't know whether to run with the crowd or stay still. His mind said run, but his little legs couldn't move. The wind from how fast people ran passed him nearly knocked him off balance. One of the runners was Kool. He threw a brown paper bag in the bushes right where Dontay was standing. Kool was fast but not fast enough. The jump-outs were right on his heels. Kool ran into the street and was hit hard by a passing car knocking him 7 feet in the air, causing him to come down on the pavement fast and hard; breaking his arm and his hip when he landed on the pavement. Dontay's eyes instantly zoomed in on the bag by the bushes. He had no clue as to what was in the bag. Whatever it was, he had no plans on sharing it with Marquise or anyone else.

As soon as he noticed that all eyes were on Kool laying on the ground, he made his move for the bag and swooped it up and put it in his pants in one swift motion without being noticed, but just when he thought the coast was clear; a familiar voice stopped him dead in his tracks. "Aye Dontay hold up."

"Shit!" He said to his self as Marquise popped up from out of the blue.

"Where you been? Why you leave me out here by myself?" He asked, then handed Marquise the $90.

"I had to take a shit. What??? You was scared or something?" He asked with a light laugh in his voice.

"Naw, I wasn't scared." He replied.

"What happened to Kool?"

"The Jump Outs came and chased him in the street and BAM! He said, slamming his fist into his hand...and just like that, the car hit him. Fucked him up too."

"Did he have the work on him?"

"I don't know, but I gotta go." Dontay turned on his heels making a fast get away out of Marquise's presence to get home to see what was in the bag that he had tucked away in his drawers.

"Damn nigga!" Marquise yelled as he stood there and watched Dontay jog across the street.

"That must was too much for him to handle in one day." He laughed to himself then served a fiend a half bag of powder as he watched Dontay fade out of his sight.

CHAPTER THREE

COMING INTO HIS OWN

"The road to success is always under construction. It is a progressive course of an endless journey."–SB

He arrived home in a matter of minutes and ran upstairs to his bedroom. He locked the door behind him and dumped what was in the paper bag onto the floor. What now lied in front of him was 200 blue baggies known as halves, with a street value of $10,000. He stood there with his right arm across his chest and his left hand on his chin contemplating how he was going to get rid of the 200 halves without Marquise knowing, because he knew Marquise wouldn't waste any time telling Kool.

The only thing that came to mind was to go back to the projects and hit the strip while Marquise slept. So without a second thought, he waited for his parents to fall asleep then got up and got dressed at 1am. He tip toed out of his room down the hall towards his parents' room and peeped inside to make sure they were asleep. His father was snoring like a bear and his mother was knocked out; dead to the world with her arms stretched out across her husband's face. Once he made it out thehouse, he got on his Mongoose bicycle and went back to the projects. At 1am, he couldn't believe how live the atmosphere was. Crowds of people were standing around everywhere. Kids as young as 7, were still riding their tricycles. The ice cream truck was still parked in the alley open for business as usual. Older dudes were running a full court basketball game, little girls were jumping Double Dutch and of course; the hustlers were spread out all throughout the projects slinging their product non-stop and no police in sight. He stood there at the recreation center and surveyed his surroundings looking for Marquise and spotted the old timer he gave the nick name Twitch, standing at the fence watching the basketball game smoking on a cigarette. He walked his bike over to where Twitch was standing.

"What's up Twitch, you seen Marquise out here?"

"Naw Shorty, Marquise don't be out here this late."

"Oh yeah, well listen. I got a deal for you."

"A Deal?" Twitch asked as he smoked his cigarette, looked Dontay up and down then straight in the eye to gauge if he was serious. He took one last drag of his cigarette then plucked it on the ground and stepped on it.

"What kind of deal you got for me?"

"If you run for me, I'll give you $10 off every half you help me sell."

"$10 huh?" Twitch asked as he stared at Dontay for a minute with a suspicious look in his eyes.

"Who coke you got...Kool's?"

Dontay was reluctant to answer for fear that Twitch already knew that Kool tossed his stash when the jump-outs chased him, and he couldn't conjure up a lie quick enough, so he remained silent. Twitched laughed "Oh I get it: Rule #1 "Never tell where you get your product from. I got you youngin. Stay right here and imma bring you the sells." Twitch agreed to run for him on the strength that he was with Marquise and Kool earlier that day not having a clue that he would be selling stolen coke that if Kool knew they had, he would have their asses laying in a dumpster for sure. Dontay let out a deep sigh of relief after Twitch agreed to help him.

That was all he needed to get him started. He bought an orange soda from the ice cream truck and posted up by the recreation center while Twitch brought him customer after customer. Money came faster than he could count it, so he stuffed every dollar into his underwear. Twitch helped him get rid of 99 of the 200 halves in 3 hours making $3900 after giving Twitch his cut. At that very moment when everything seemed to be going as smooth as he could have dreamed, the unexpected grabbed him by the throat when a tall, slim built older guy approached Twitch in an aggressive manner with the look of death in his eyes. "Where the fuck is that muthafuckin coke at nigga?!" His voice was deep, raspy, and full of anger. He was dressed in all black with a hoody over his head to try and obscure as much of his identity as possible but Dontay could see the thick razor cut on the gunman's right cheek.

He locked his eyes on the long barrel of the 12 gauge shot gun that the gunman had pointed right at Twitch's face and he instantly felt a strong urge to piss.

"I know you up here selling them *blue* baggies nigga, where the fuck are they? I'm not gonna ask you no mu'fuckin' more nigga, where the fuck is them *blue* bags at?" Twitch tried to speak, but his fear caused his Tourettes' to kick in full gear and he began to twitch and stutter uncontrollably. Without a moment's notice, the sound of the shot gun blast sent people running and screaming in a frenzy. Dontay couldn't believe his eyes. Twitch's headless body fell limp to the ground. Dontay dropped his soda, grabbed his bike and got outta there. He peddled as fast as his little legs would move; like Lance Armstrong in the Tour de France until he was back home.

He wasn't expecting anyone to be awake in his house at 4am, when he snuck back in using his key as quietly as he could to avoid making a sound. But little did he know, his father was in the kitchen looking in the refrigerator for a late night snack, when he heard the squeaky sound of the front door opening. Thinking it may be a burglar, he grabbed the baseball bat from the pantry and tip-toed towards the front door. He had the bat gripped tight, cocked over his shoulder and ready to swing at the first head he saw. He reached the hallway and turned on the light only to see his son startled by the unexpectancy of the bright lights. The relief he felt when he saw it was just his dad and not his mother caused him to exhale.

"Boy! I almost Babe Ruthed your shit to the moon and knocked your little head clean off your body. What the hell are you doing coming in here at 4 in the god-damned morning?"

Dontay was breathing hard and could hardly speak. He grabbed the side of his head with both hands and sat on the floor by the door as he replayed Twitch getting shot in the face over and over and over again. "What's wrong? His dad asked with a concerned tone in his voice and a curious look on his face, still wondering why his 11 year old son was coming in the house at 4am and sitting on the floor holding his head. "I was up Montana and…"

"HOLD UP! You was where?"

"Don't tell Ma, but, I went up Montana to hustle and I saw somebody get their head blown off."

"To hustle huh? What your young ass know about hustling?"

"I found some halves, and I just wanted to make some money to help Ma out around the house with the bills and stuff. Twitch was only helping me and he got shot in the face for nothing. I'm never going back up there again."

His father saw that his young son had the tenacity and ambition to follow in his footsteps, but lacked the fortitude to be able to stomach the bloodshed that came along with the business; and the knowledge of the game to be able to survive in them streets. He felt it was only right to educate him before he made the decision to give it up before he even got started.

"Listen to me son! First and foremost: DON'T EVER tell anyone what you saw cause we don't need anyone coming around here looking for you. Rule #1: YOU NEVER TELL...you understand?" Dontay shook his head yeah then waited for further instructions from his dad.

"Let me tell you a little something about hustling." He sat down on the floor beside his son and put his arm over his shoulder.

"You gonna see all kinds of shit out there in them streets. You gotta have the fortitude to be strong enough to stomach the violence that comes along with that way of the life. You gotta leave your feelings outta that game, and show no weakness if you wanna be a hustler and be able to survive out there in them streets because they will devour the weak. You understand? People respect a hustler, but they fear violence. You gonna learn as you progress in the game that in some circumstances, violence is necessary, but try as you might to keep the money and murder separate because when the bodies start dropping, the feds will come knocking...and knocking hard. Everything you worked to establish will be gone like that."

He demonstrated how quickly he could lose everything if he wasn't careful by snapping his finger.

Dontay was happy that his dad was so understanding, unaware that the education he just received came from firsthand experience. He continued to drop jewels on his son about the game until Dontay fell asleep. He picked up his young son, carried him to his room and laid him down on the bed. As he removed his son's shoes and pants, he noticed the huge bulge in his son's underwear. He pulled back the waist band and removed the wad of cash and brown paper bag containing 100 *blue* baggies of coke. He counted the money and stared at his son while he slept. A slight smirk crept onto his face as he thought to himself how he would groom his son to become his heir and one of the best hustlers the city ever saw.

He laid the money on the top of the night stand, and put the baggies in his pocket. The last thing he wanted was for his son to get eaten alive by the vultures in the streets before he had a chance to show him the ropes on how to survive out there. He took the 100 *blue* baggies of coke to one of his runners on Hanover Place, where he reigned supreme. He was known as **KING** because of his sheer dominance and constant flow of narcotics that he pumped into the streets...not to mention, **KING** was the English translation of his birth name Rey.

CHAPTER FOUR

EARLY LESSONS

"The game of life only has one rule: ALWAYS WIN!"–SB

The next morning Dontay woke up to the aroma of fresh pancakes. He stretched his arms, then reached down inside his underwear and discovered the paper bag full of money and drugs wasn't there. He jumped up in a frantic and threw back the covers on his bed. Nothing was there. "Shit!" He said, then took a deep exhaled sigh of relief when he saw the money neatly stacked on his nightstand, but was puzzled as to where the coke was. "Dad!" Was the first thing that came to mind, preparing for what could possibly be the worse ass whippin' of his young life if his dad told his mother. He hid the money inside a shoebox in his closet, took a shower, got dressed and walked into the kitchen as if he was walking to the electric chair. Slow and steady, preparing himself for what's to come. His mother was at the stove when he entered and his father was sitting at the table reading the Washington Times newspaper. He pulled out a chair and sat down, staring at his father for the slightest indication that he was in the worse trouble of his young life.

"Good morning son." She said when she heard him walk in and sat a plate of buttermilk pancakes and scrambled eggs and bacon in front of him, while rubbing his head. Her pleasant sentiment indicated that she was in a good mood, and that his father hadn't mentioned a word to her about their conversation. However, he was still unable to get a read on how his father really felt because he remained silent and he never looked up from his newspaper.

"Good morning Ma."

"Did you sleep well son?" She asked as she walked back to the sink and began washing dishes.

"Yeah Ma'am. I slept o.k." He answered through a mouth full of food, periodically peeping over at his father.

His mother continued to make small talk about her new Avon products and how her customers loved that peach lipstick, and his father never uttered a word or took his eyes off the newspaper. Just as Dontay took his last bite and put his fork down, his father stood up and folded the newspaper under his armpit.

"Come on, let's go. Imma give you a ride to school this morning." He said.

Dontay didn't know what to think of the unexpected change in the order of how things went in his household, but wouldn't dare question it.

Things seemed out of the ordinary, and all he could think about was his father finding that coke in his draws and wanted to give him another lecture on the game. Once they were inside the car, his dad put him at ease when he told him that before he took him to school, he was going to give him a little education about the game and show him how real hustlers play this game of life. He turned the key in the ignition and the loud roar of the Diamond Jubilee 460 CID V8 engine inside of the 1978 Lincoln Mark 5 caused Dontay to smile with excitement. Whenever he was able to spend time with his dad was a joyful moment for him. King was the youngest of 11 siblings to poor avocado farmer parents in the Dominican Republic. He grew up having to share the milk in the cereal bowl with his brothers and sisters.

By the age of 8, he began cultivating the land in the field and began working as a marijuana guard to raise money for his struggling family. By the age of 18 on his way back from school, he was confronted by a squad of police that told him that his entire family had all died in a house fire when the local vigilantes wanted to send a message after his dad refused to give up his land. Young King packed his bags and fled to the United States, where he fell in love and married Dontay's mom; and was proud to have a son. King was Dontay's hero. He loved his dad and wanted to be just like him. "So you wanna be a hustler huh?"His dad asked. "Yeah!"

His father looked over at him with a smile of a proud father then turned on the radio. The sound of James Brown's "Poppa don't take no Mess" came through the speakers as he pulled out of the parking space.

Dontay sat back in his father's Lincoln Mark V barely able to look out of the window, but enjoyed every bit of the view he was able to see as they drove through parts of the city that he had never seen before. They made a left on North Capital and traveled slowly past the carry-out and liquor store where a large crowd of people lined the entire sidewalk. His dad waved to a few hustlers on the corner then made a right turn on Hanover Place, a narrow street with barely any room for the car to drive down due to the large crowd of people scattered throughout the street. The crowd parted like the Red Sea when the Lincoln drove down the street. Everyone knew who's car it was "That's King!" One lady yelled out from the sidewalk and everyone showed him respect when he came through. Women looked like prostitutes, dressed in their leather miniskirts, sequin blouses, and thigh high, high heeled boots. Gangsters and hustlers all showed respect as he slowly drove up the strip.

He glanced over at his son and said "Rule #2: Trust No One. This right here, where we are now is the strip. A lot of money is being made right here on this little street. This is where I conduct my business."

"You a hustler dad?"

"Yeah, I guess you can call it that, but I like to use the term entrepreneur."

"What's an entrepreneur?" Dontay asked.

"An entrepreneur is a boss who works for himself, one who organizes the structure of the business; as well as the one who assumes all the risk of profits and losses. If you wanna be an entrepreneur, it's a lot you need to know about people, about business and about these streets. The moment you treat this business like it's a game, you already lost."

As King began to educate his young son on street law and economics, he caught the mean mug stare from a strange looking guy that he never saw before standing on the opposite side of the street at the edge of the alley wearing a hooded sweat shirt and smoking a cigarette.

He wondered if the man in the hoody was someone from his past, the police, a stick-up boy or just another nigga that couldn't make a dollar on the strip as long as the heroin they called "brown tape" was on the block. King signaled for one of his workers to come over.

"What's up Boss?" The worker named Rob asked as he leaned up against the passenger side door and handed King a stack of cash.

"No need to count it Boss, it's all there." King put the cash inside the glove compartment, then asked" Who's the clown by the alley

51

with the hoody on?" Rob peeped over the rim of his shades to get a clear look.

"I don't know, I never seen him before. You want me to handle it?"

"Naw, keep it peaceful around here and get money. We don't need the strip shut down and swarming with cops, you dig me?"

"Alright Boss." Rob said as he stepped away from the car and glanced back over his shoulder at King, then over at the guy standing in the alleyway.

"One of the keys to survival out here in these streets is to always be aware of your surroundings, always pay attention to what's said and what's going on around you at all times."

King glanced over at his son and said "That money in the glove compartment is yours. I had my man get rid of it for you because it's a lot you need to learn before you get too far ahead of yourself." King made a U-turn to leave Hanover and noticed the man with the hoody as looking up at the rooftop of the house, on the opposite side of the street. He gave the shooter that was positioned on the roof with the eagle scope 30-R6 rifle the signal to stand down, using the finger across the neck. He took one last drag of his cigarette, plucked it to the ground and then walked away. King looked back in the direction of the alley where the man in the hoody was standing only to see two fiends fumbling with their work. He had a sharp sense of observation, and was always prepared to deal with whatever the situation entailed.

He looked over at his son with a grin on his face. "That's enough for now, you gotta get to school before your mother kills me." Dontay sat in silence, taking in the smell and nefariousness of the atmosphere.

"Dad, can I ask you something?"

"Yeah son, you can ask me anything."

"Why they call you King?"

"King is the English word for my name Rey. So instead of using my real name out here in these streets, I use what you would call a pseudonym, a fake name." As he drove, he continued to give his son the law of the life but, periodically glanced up at the rearview mirror and noticed he was being followed. Two occupants in a black Pontiac GTO had been following him since he pulled off of Hanover Place. King quickly dismissed the tail as the police because they didn't drive Pontiacs. He readjusted the rearview mirror to get a better look at their faces and the closer they got, he instantly recognized the passenger as the man in the hoody by the alley.

King took the side streets to try to lose the tail but they followed him turn for turn. He wanted to get his son somewhere safe and out of harm's way just in case things got out of hand. Within minutes, he pulled up at his son's school, never taking his eyes off the rearview mirror. The tail stopped a car length behind him. King looked over at his son and slid the .38 caliber pistol from under the driver's seat and placed it on his lap.

"Have a good day at school son, and make sure you come straight home because it's something

I need to show you."

"OK, Dad." Dontay said as he opened the car door and got out. King looked back at the rearview mirror and saw the passenger of the car walking towards the Lincoln, putting his hoody on his head. Before the car door could close shut when his son exited the vehicle, the door flung open and the man with the hoody got in with his gun pointed at King's face but King's Intuition had him on point and ready for the move and had his gun cocked and aimed.

Dontay looked back towards the car as he made his way up the steps towards the entrance of the school.

"I don't know who sent you, but your first mistake was getting your ass in my car." Before the assassin could say a word, one shot from King's gun hit him point blank range in the stomach. He returned fire with his .45 caliber pistol hitting King once in the chest. The impact knocked King up against the driver's side door fast and hard. King was still alive but too weak from the bullet in his chest to raise his gun. He's gasping for air. The assassin was also in excruciating pain from the shot to his gut, but managed to gather up enough strength to raise his gun and put an end to the man known in the streets as "King" with a single shot to the temple... **BLOA!**

Dontay stood there traumatized at what he just saw. Everything seemed to be moving in slow motion as he witnessed his father get murdered right in front of him.

The assassin was in too much pain to move, so he sat there momentarily with his hand pressed up against the gun-shot wound in his stomach to try to stop the bleeding. "Shit!" He said as he began to get hot. He removed the hoody from off his head as sweat began to pour down his forehead.

His partner got out of the driver's seat of the Lincoln in haste to save him. He rushed to the passenger's side door and pulled him out. Dontay was still in a trance while the assassin exited the Lincoln. He looked in Dontay's direction and tried to muster up the strength to raise his gun, but was too weak. Dontay didn't flinch. He stared at the assassin's face and instantly noticed the cut on the right side of it and had a brief flash back of Twitch getting shot... "Scar!" He said to himself. His partner put Scar's arm over his shoulder for leverage.

"The kid, kill the kid!" Scar ordered. His partner pulled his gun from his waist, aimed it at Dontay and fired one shot. The bullet missed, and in that instance, the entrance door flung open and Dontay was pulled inside by the janitor.

"Are you alright?" He asked. Dontay in a state of shock remained silent.

Scar's partner helped him to the car, laid him in the back seat and sped off. The janitor rushed Dontay to the office "Call the police!" He yelled to the secretary sitting at the desk. "Someone just got killed outside and shot at this kid."

He sat Dontay down in the chair by the door and knelt down beside him. "Was that your dad in the car?" Dontay sat there in complete silence, shocked and traumatized. Voices were muffled, his vision was a little blurry and everything seemed to be moving in slow motion. He felt anger for the first time in his young life at it's highest form. This was the second time Scar had impacted his life with killing someone close to him. Although he only knew Twitch a short period of time, he liked him and he felt responsible for his death by giving him the blue bags to sell that Scar killed him so easily over, but this one was far more personal. He vowed to himself that if ever he saw Scar again when he got older, he would do him the same way he did Twitch and his dad or worse.

The police arrived on the scene and quickly began questioning everyone for potential witnesses. No one saw anything but heard the gunshots loud and clear as if they were right there in the school's hallway. Homicide detectives approached Dontay while he sat quietly and still in a state of shock.

"Hey kid, how you doing?" The detective asked. He pulled out his pen and pad and attempted to ask Dontay a barrage of questions that fell on deaf ears. The sound of his mother's voice in the distance snapped him out of his trance. He slowly turned his head and saw his mother making her way through the commotion. She rushed to his side

"Are you OK?" She asked then hugged him tight. She grabbed his hand "Come on, let's go!

"Ma'am, my name is Detective Smith and I have a few more questions to ask your son if you don't mind."

"I do mind!" She snapped back. "My son don't know nothing, and it's against the law to question a minor without his parents."

"Ma'am your son may be in more danger than you know. One of the assassins responsible for your husband's death was heard saying "kill the boy" then he was shot at."

"And, here you are trying to put him in even more danger by being seen talking to YOU!"

"We can help!"

"Help how? By questioning a kid about a murder? Put him on the stand so whoever killed his father can get his friends to kill my son, to keep him from talking? You really don't have a fucking clue about the code of the streets, do you detective? Do yourself a favor, help your own family and I'll take care of mines."

Holding her son's hand, she turned her back to Detective Smith and walked away. He watched her closely as she led her son through the crowd of spectators towards the exit. Detective Smith thought to himself, her attitude seemed strange and rather peculiar for someone whose husband was just murdered right in front of their son. He wondered if she had some involvement, and made a mental note to himself to check her financial records to see if any life insurance policy existed.

Tears rolled down her face as soon as she stepped outside of the school and walked pass the crime scene. She tried with all her might not to lose her cool in front of the crowd of teachers watching her every step, and not once did she look at her husband's dead body as the medical examiners put King in the coroner's van. Detective Smith stepped out of the building with a deeply suspicious look in his eyes as he watched her closely until she turned the corner and was out of his sight.

She stopped as soon as she turned the corner and noticed that she was now out of sight of the police and dropped to her knees. She let out a painful sigh from the feeling of losing the one man that she ever loved, but knew that the life he lived would one day catch up with him. She cursed him with anger for leaving her. Tears poured down her cheeks as she hugged her son tight.

Dontay had never seen his mother in so much pain before. She had always been the rock of his family. He never heard her complain. She was always the strongest, and never let adversity get the best of her. She always found a way to make sure her family was good. So to see her in this moment of weakness, was just as much of a shock to him as it was to witness his father's death.

She broke their embrace, put her hands on his shoulders and kissed him on the forehead.

"I'm just thankful to God that you're alright." She kissed him again.

"I seen who did it." Dontay said.

"You what?!"

"I seen him. This man I call Scar, that's who killed Dad." His mother held him by the shoulders and looked him in his eyes.

"Promise me two things son! Promise me you'll never tell no one what you saw, and I mean NO one! You hear me?!" He shook his head in the affirmative. "And promise me that you won't ever follow in your father's footsteps. I can't lose the one and only love I have left to these streets." "I promise Ma." Dontay replied.

She grabbed him by his face and kissed him again on his forehead. Then stood up, grabbed his hand and proceeded home. She accepted King's way of life, and loved him unconditionally regardless of what he was involved in. She had prepared herself for this day a long time ago, but the pain was unbearable. She prayed every single night that this day would never come, but God had other plans for King, and his will always supersedes prayers.

She tried to hold her composure together as best she could, but the pain of losing the only man she ever loved, hurt deeper than she revealed on the outside and she refused to allow her only son to die in the streets like some animal. Little did she know, Dontay had other plans in mind.

CHAPTER FIVE

She threw the car in park, got out in one swift motion, and ran as fast as she could into the emergency room screaming for help "I have someone who's been shot in my car, I need help!"

The nurse and EMT rushed out and put Scar on the gurney, speeding him back into the emergency room. Several hours passed and Pearl's nerves were a wreck. She raised Scar since he was 7 and she was only 16, when both of their parents died from an apparent drug overdose. Doctor Wilson exited the operating room, removing his gloves and approached Pearl sitting in the waiting room.

"Excuse me miss, are you a relative of Mr. White?"

"Yes, I'm his sister. Is he OK?"

"The operation was successful. He'll survive...

"Thank God!" Pearl said.

However, he suffered a very serious gunshot at close range that ruptured both his small and large intestines, which will require him to wear a colostomy bag for quite some time until his intestines heal and become strong enough to function on their own, but he'll live."

"Thank you so much Doc."

"You're very welcome, but before you can go in to see him, there are a couple of detectives here to ask you a few questions."

"Detectives! I told you he was shot at the park by a robber."

"Yes, I know but they just wanna get a statement from you."

Within minutes, the detectives approached Pearl and began to throw a barrage of questions at her. Since they had no report of gun shots in the area, they took Pearl's statement and description of what the fake robber looked like but in Pearl's twisted way of playing mind games, she thought it would be quite funny to give them a fake description of a white man; since in one way or another they always seemed to blame a black man for everything.

She wanted to see just how much they really paid attention to detail or were they just going through with their procedure. Her description was of the detective taking the notes. Tall white male 6'3'' in height, heavy set about 285lbs., Blond hair with a thick mustache and glasses.

"OK Miss, we got it! We'll get right on it and send out an all points bulletin for the perpetrator."

"Thank you so much detectives, you're so helpful." She said shaking her head at exactly what she suspected about how black victims were treated in Montgomery County.

After their report inquiry the detectives turned and left the hospital. Pearl watched them until they were out of her sight and laughed to herself at the mind game she'd played on them.

"Big fat sloppy stupid mu'fuckaz." She spat then walked into the operating room only to see

Scar out of it from the anesthesia. There were tubes in his mouth, his nose, his stomach, and I.V's in both arms.

"Damn Baby, who did this to you?" She rubbed his head and leaned forward to kiss him on the cheek.

"I'm not going nowhere, I'll be here when you wake up little brother." Four hours later, the anesthesia was beginning to wear off. Scar opened his eyes, feeling a little groggy and still in agonizing pain. He saw his sister asleep in the chair and smiled at the sight of her. After weeks in the hospital, Scar was discharged and allowed to go home with strict instructions to remain on bed rest for another 2 months.

A HUSTLER'S AMBITION

"Action is what ignites success. Action is what produces results. Knowledge in the mind of someone who knows how to put his plan into action with intellect over emotions will be successful in his own right."–SB

Some time had passed since Dontay witnessed his father's murder. He was now a teenager and determined to make his name known in the streets amongst the city's most ruthless, while attempting to find the men responsible for his father's death. At the same time, get as much money as possible.

After being away from the projects for some time, he eventually made his way back to where it all began. He carefully observed his surroundings and watched a young hustler name Rocko collect stacks after stacks of money from his runners. The block was pumpin' and Rocko counted paper non-stop. Rocko was still that young, flamboyant hustler who had it all. Nice cars, fly clothes, every sneaker that was popular, and expensive jewelry. All the girls in the neighborhood who wanted to be with him and all the niggas in the neighborhood wanting to be like him. Rocko was that neighborhood superstar. The nigga that your mother warned you to stay away from.

He was standing in the alley by the basketball court getting his XJS Jaguar coupe washed when Dontay got up the nerve and approached him.

"What's up Rocko? Is this your car?" Dontay asked in admiration as he looked inside.

"Yeah, this my car, but get your nosey ass eyes up out of it." Rocko said as he glanced up momentarily, then proceeded to count his money.

"No disrespect. I just like it that's all." Dontay said as he glided his hand across the hood. "How much you pay for this joint?"

Rocko laughed at the young Dontay's inquiry. "Why? You want one?"

"Naw, I want two!"

"Two huh?"

"Damn Right! When I get rich, Imma get a black and a white one."

"Get rich huh?" Rocko asked as he studied Dontay carefully. It was something about this kid that he liked. How he talked about getting rich was different from the conversations he heard from the youngins his age that only wanted sneaker money. His ambition wasn't like that of your average 16 year old. He could tell that Dontay was serious about wanting the long term riches.

"Alright, you think you can handle an ounce?" Dontay, being naïve to the mass and weight break down of the metric system, didn't have a clue what an ounce was but was confident that he could sell it after his brief stint in the game thanks to Marquise.

"Yeah, I can handle an ounce but Imma need a little more than that because I got a couple friends that wanna hustle too. An ounce ain't gonna be enough for all three of us to see some real money."

"Some real money huh! Oh I forgot, you wanna get rich and buy two Jags." Rocko said with a bit of sarcasm in his voice and a grin on his face. He stared at Dontay for a minute and could see the seriousness in his young eyes. "O.K., wait right here." Rocko walked away without saying another word and went inside an apartment building. Within minutes he returned carrying an Athlete's Foot Bag. He didn't tell Dontay what was in it, and Dontay knew better than to ask. He ordered Dontay with a hand gesture to get in the car and without hesitation, Dontay was in the passenger's seat.

"Aiight shorty, check this out. Imma see just how much of a hustler you really are. Imma give you a chance to prove yourself with an 8th of a key for $3,500 since you say you want some real money. If you sell it right without taking any shorts, you should make close to $9,000, and that's a pretty good start for a 16 year old if you ask me."

The sound of 9G's was like hitting the lottery but, he never forgot the jewel his father told him about being your own boss and assuming your own risk with your profits and losses. This is a business, not a game.

"Take me home real quick." Dontay said. Within minutes, Rocko turned on New York Ave and pulled up at Dontay's house.

Dontay could barely wait for the car to come to a complete stop. He jumped out and ran in the house and up to his room as fast as he could. He counted out $3,500 that he had stashed away inside his shoes and slid down the banister of the steps; jetted out the door and jumped off the porch. Within seconds he was back in the front seat of Rocko's Jag and handed him the shoe box.

"Here you go." Dontay said and sat the shoe box on Rocko's lap.

"What's this?" Rocko asked before taking the top off the box.

"That's the $3,500 for the 8th." Rocko lifted the lid of the shoe box and looked inside and smiled at what he saw. He looked at Dontay with an impressed look in his eyes then shook his head in agreement at the youngin's ambition. His intuition about him was right. This youngin' was different from all the rest and Rocko knew at that very moment, he had found his young prodigy. Rocko pulled off without saying a word and was at his apartment in a matter of minutes. Dontay looked around in admiration of the décor as soon as he crossed the threshold.

the two that went hand-to-hand would switch with the two that were on look out. They pumped their work around the clock, going hand to hand; selling half after half until they were dead tired. They would even fall asleep outside not wanting to miss a sell. Not allowing a single dollar to pass them by. Rocko watched from the sideline like a proud coach as his young team of dynamite young hustlers jumped in the life and grinded with non-stop persistence.

They sold every half and stacked up $36,000. The most money any of them had ever seen in their young lives. Just when things were going smooth for them, Rocko became the victim of an undercover drug bust.

Unsure of his next move, Dontay met with his team to discuss their plans moving forward and they all agreed to bury the money in his back yard where only he knew where it was. He would leave it buried until he found a way to re-up and flip their paper. Dontay had real millionaire dreams and wasn't going to let nothing or no one stop him. He vowed to bring that dream to fruition by all means.

With Rocko locked up, Dontay had to result to other measures and learn different methods of hustling in order to build up his arsenal of knowledge about the many elements of the hustle. It's one thing to be just a **"STREET NIGGA"** but it's something totally different to be a **"NIGGA IN THE STREETS."** The difference is simple. A street nigga is one who is just outside running the streets with no sense of direction or any knowledge of who is who, or what is what in the many facets of the streets; or any knowledge of the dangers that lurk in other elements that he or she may have no understanding of. The saying "You never send a boy to do a man's job" is true in this case. You can't send a man that kills for a living to conduct business on a major level to a connect for 100 bricks. Certain skills have to be acquired first. Certain mannerisms, certain lingo and etiquette have to be taught. Dontay understood that to be a nigga in the streets, means you can adapt quickly to any situation and understand every element and every walk of life because you're out there knee deep in the trenches; breathing it, eating it, and living it every single day and night. This is your job...your life. Nothing else matters and you will let nothing or no one stand in your way to become who you set out to be. Your word and your reputation becomes just as much a part of you as your very own skin.

Dontay tried his hand in the pill game and invested $5,000 on 500 Dilaudids also known as D's on the Northwest side of the city. He copped D's at $10 per pill and resold them for $35 a pill, banking in $17,500; a quick profit of $12,500 and bringing his bottom line to a total of $48,500. He put the $5,000 back in the stash and split the

$12,000 with is crew, giving them $3,000 a piece to keep 'em happy until things picked up. Like Rocko told him, you ain't really about that paper if it ain't enough to share with your team. The experience of selling D's uptown on 10th & V street N.W., introduced Dontay to a different kind of addict, and a more sophisticated way of hustling. He learned the value of street economics, marketing and finance. Buy low and sell high.

He learned the business side of the trade and knew exactly what it was going to take in order to secure his seat at the table amongst the city's best and most respected hustlers.

The "Crack Epidemic" exploded on the scene all across American cities before anyone could prepare for it. Fiends were popping up from everywhere, coming from all walks of life. Crack cocaine dramatically increased the number of addicts 5 to 1, more than there was with powder cocaine.

The money started to flow too fast to hide it all. Dontay and his crew were sitting on a hefty amount of cash but it wasn't close to enough for him to do what he planned.

While lying in bed with his hands crossed behind his head and staring up at the ceiling, he contemplated on who he could re-up with. The thought crossed his mind to go holla at one of his father's old partners on Hanover Place, but it wasn't time to show his face to them yet and reveal to them who he was. Besides, he didn't know who he could trust or who was involved with his father's murder so he quickly dismissed the idea as fast as he thought of it and fell asleep.

CHAPTER SEVEN

HUSTLIN' 101

"There is no such thing as luck. All you have is preparation that leads to opportunity."—SB

The next day after school, Dontay went to a female hustler's house in the Montana housing project named Ronetta. She was 5 years his senior and the female version of him. She hustled out of her house 24/7 and was on a serious paper chase. Ronetta was all about the money. If you weren't talking money, she had no conversation for you. While sitting on the couch counting his cash, he noticed a unfamiliar face stroll pass him eating a sandwich; revealing his gold teeth and wearing one of the biggest gold rope chains he had ever seen. "This nigga gotta to be from New York" He said to himself. He put his money back in his pocket and yelled for Ronetta.

She knew something was wrong from the tone in which he used when he called her. "Boy, what! Why the hell you yelling up in here like you ain't got no damn sense?" "Who the fuck is that nigga with the gold teeth?" "That's Donavon from New York." She said.

"NEW YORK! Hold the fuck up Ro. That's what we doing now? You letting New Yorkers hustle up outta here now."

"Boy, the last time I checked, this was my mu'fuckin' house don't be coming up in here like you run shit! Them niggaz is good peoples, plus they got the biggest 50's I ever seen." She said as she held out her hand with a 50 rock the size of a Now and Later piece of candy.

"Got damn! They selling all that for 50?"

"Yeah, now you see why I let these niggaz parlay up in here. This right here is what they call crack. This that new shit that got these mu'fuckaz out here geeking like shit. They do anything for this shit. Nigga, they'll sell their babies for this shit. Just one of these pay my mu'fuckin' rent and my mu'fuckin' car note, so you got to be out your rabbit ass mind if you think Imma let you or anybody else run these niggaz off. You see this?" She pulled out a .44 Bulldog revolver and held it by her face with the barrel pointed towards the ceiling. "Yeah, 44 nigga, and imma bust a cap in any niggaz ass around this bitch if they get in the way of my money. Believe that!"

Dontay stared at the pistol in Ronetta's hand, and thought... **"This bitch is crazy!"** However, it might not be a bad move to holla at the New Yorkers to flip his money. He didn't know anything about crack but with Ronetta on his team, he couldn't lose.

He walked out of Ronetta's house looking for the New Yorker and caught a sudden movement out the corner of his eye of someone peeping their head around the corner of the building.

Dontay slowly approached the edge of the building with caution. The closer he got, he began to hear voices.

"Take that shit off bitch ass nigga and rabbit ear them pockets. Hurry the fuck up nigga fo' I buss your mu'fuckin' head open, and kick them shoes over here too."

Dontay slowly walked around the edge of the building and saw the New Yorkers getting robbed at gun point with their pants down around their ankles by his aunt's boyfriend, Clean.

Clean was a known jack boy in the hood. Straight stick up nigga that was coming to get it if he didn't respect you or felt like you weren't man enough to hold your own.

Clean's attention quickly turned to Dontay when he came around the corner.

"What's up nephew, grab them shoes right there." He directed Dontay towards the shoes on the ground with the barrel of the pistol.

"What the fuck is you doing C? Man, them my peoples right there." Clean turned and looked at Dontay in disbelief. "Your peoples??? Nigga get the fuck outta here, these ain't your peoples."

"Bullshit aside slim, them my peoples from New York right there. They wit me!"

Clean turned and looked at Dontay still with a look of disbelief in his eyes, and couldn't believe he was getting in his business like that. Dontay knew he was dead ass wrong for getting in the way of Clean's move, but he saw the bigger picture, and told himself that he would explain it to clean later.

Clean lowered his gun and tucked it away in the waistband of his pants. He stared at Dontay for a minute, then looked at the New Yorkers and walked away without saying another word.

"YO!" The New Yorker named Donovan said in his Trinidadian accent as he pulled his pants up and put his shoes back on his feet. The other New Yorker name Romincio remained quiet; as he too pulled his pants up and held his necklace in his hand.

"Yo kid, I appreciate that son. That was some real shit right there kid. If you need "ANYTHING." I mean anything, holla at me!" Donovan said.

"Word!" You don't know us from a hole in the wall and you stepped up for us. That's love right there kid... here you go." Romincio said as he tossed Dontay his gold rope chain with the lion's head medallion the size of his fist.

"Naw you can keep that. That's not my style! I wanna holla at you about them boulders y'all got. I'm trying to get money."

The sound of the car horn caused Dontay to peep out the window through the blinds to see the burgundy rental car with Donovan in the driver's seat. Dontay casually walked out of Ronetta's house and got in the passenger's seat.

"You got a lot of respect around here son. Ro couldn't stop talkin' bout you. We got something real nice planned for you for what you did for us."

Within minutes they pulled up at the Master Host Hotel on New York Avenue. Inside the room was Romincio and another guy that Dontay never saw before. At the sight of Dontay walking through the door, Romincio got up off the bed and embraced him as if they knew each other their entire life.

"Aye Yo Blue, Dis the kid I was tellin' you bout." Romincio said. Blue sat at the bed and was engaging in a conversation on the phone when Dontay walked in.

He glanced up at him when Romincio embraced him.

"How old are you?" Blue asked as he hung up the phone.

"16" Dontay replied.

"16! You look like you're 10."

Romincio started laughing. "Yeah, he might look like he's 10 but he got the respect in the hood like a grown man.

"This kid can't run no block." Blue said.

"Don't jump to conclusions so fast bro. I'm telling you, if you would've seen how he got the older cat to back off us, you wouldn't be saying that. Trust me on this. This kid got potential."

Romincio gave Blue a look of reassurance trying to convince him to trust his judgment in Dontay's character.

"I don't know about this." Blue said. Romincio approached Blue and whispered "Listen, this is who we need to get into these projects. If we got any chance of getting a piece of that gold mine up Montana Terrace, we need this kid to be our conduit to some major paper in this town. Think about it. We might can get 20 g's for a bird in New York, but we can definitely get 20 to 22 g's easy down here."

Blue stared at Romincio for a minute, looked over his shoulder at Dontay, then back at Romincio... "This is on you. He's your responsibility."

"O.K. dig this, this what imma do. Imma try you out. Right on cue Romincio tossed him a small shopping bag. Dontay caught the bag with both hands.

"What's this?"

"Didn't I tell you I was gonna bless you!" Romincio said.

"Yeah, but..."

"Ain't no but." Romincio cut him off in mid sentence..."One of the things you gonna learn about me is when I give my word, I keep it. So that's the blessing I told you I was gonna give you. That right there is 36 ounces. 1 Kilo. You owe me 20 grand."

"You think you can handle all that?" were the doubtful words that came out of Blue's mouth.

Without saying a word, Dontay rolled up the bag and tucked it away in his pants.

"I'll call you in a couple days." He looked at Romincio and headed out the door.

"You want a ride?" Donovan asked.

"Naw, I can walk from here."

As soon as he got out of the door he took off running towards Queens Chapel Road. Jogged another two blocks over the bridge and was at the front door of his mother's house in no time.

Dontay called Marquise and made another attempt to pull him into his circle, and again, he rejected his invitation to join his crew. He insisted that Dontay was only a pawn for the New Yorkers and that he would never work for a nigga that he introduced to the hustle, then hung up. Dontay looked at the phone in disbelief then put it down on the hook. Dontay was shocked at Marquise's sudden change in attitude towards him and contributed it to jealousy of his come up.

He picked up the phone and began to dial numbers. He called the ones he knew would be down to follow his lead no matter where he took them. C.C., Dan, Pat, Lil Crip, Terry and Calvin. He told them to meet him at Ronetta's house. Once everyone was there, they went to the table and got Ronnetta to show them exactly how big the $20 rocks were suppose to be and went to work chopping up every ounce in the kilo. When they finished, they cut up 3,600/$20 rocks and went straight to work. The order was to take no shorts and to bring all money back to Ronetta. They pumped all night into the early morning and got rid of the whole brick hand to hand in a day and a half and couldn't wait to see the look on Blue's face when he gave him his money.

The call to Blue was made as soon as they counted all the money, all $72,000 of it. He separated Blue's from theirs and still ended up with a hefty $52,000. He gave his team $5,000 a piece and put the other $27,000 in the stash spot to go back and re-up with. Dontay didn't take a cut out the money. His plan was to stack every dollar he made to position himself for a bigger come up. When the time came for him to meet Blue and give him his money, the look on Blue's face was priceless. He could tell that Blue was impressed and didn't expect Dontay to be finished and have his money so fast.

All Dontay wanted was to make one hell of a statement. He wanted to show that he was just as good of a hustler, if not better than anyone Blue knew; and he did a hell of a job putting himself in the

CHAPTER EIGHT

Unsure of where to go or what to do, he wandered around the projects for a moment until a voice caught his attention from behind him.

"What you gonna do with that?" Dontay turned around and was relieved to see Blue standing there holding his gun and wiping the sweat from off his forehead.

"I don't know what I was gonna do, but I wanted to make sure you was alright."

Blue smiled at Dontay's attempt to come to his aid, and at that very moment, a friendship was formed.

A trip that was only meant to be for the weekend turned out to be a month, and on the eve of Blue's birthday they decided to go shopping in SoHo for furniture and other house accessories for Blue's new studio apartment in Crown Heights. Dontay quickly noticed the change in Blue's demeanor, and zoomed in on where Blue's attention went. He felt like he had just walked into the middle of a Mexican standoff. Blue on one end, and another guy on the other. Staring at each other with the look of death in their eyes, neither one saying a word. Just stares and mean mugs said enough. They hated each other, but now wasn't the time or place to get into an O.K. Corral type shootout. Dontay paid close attention to both men's demeanor and watched the other guy's every move until he walked away and was now out of sight.

"Who was that?" Dontay asked.

"Remember I got into the shootout? Well, that was him."

Dontay looked back to see if there was any sign of him trying to double back and bring them a move from behind with the element of surprise. He had blended in with the crowd of shoppers and there was no sign of him. A sense of uneasiness began to take over him, and he was starting to show more signs of caution than Blue. He watched everyone closely, paying more attention to his surroundings like his dad once told him was the key to surviving in these streets. Blue began to laugh and joke as if he never saw the guy that was shooting at him the other night. Dontay's nerves calmed down once they made it to the Holly Golighty area to do some more shopping on Fifth Ave in Manhattan, where they grabbed a bite to eat at E &E grill house on W. 49th near Broadway.

Over the course of the month that Dontay spent in New York, he got cool with a few young hustlers his age from Albany projects and Flatbush Ave, named Fat Ham and Supreme. Supreme gave Dontay a small .38 revolver pistol to carry while they hustled in and around the projects at night. They made frequent trips back and forth to the Bodega while they grind for snacks. On their way back, they laughed and joked on each other as they made their way towards a small group huddled up playing Cee-lo.

Dontay's heart instantaneously began beating faster than usual when he and the guy shaking the dice made eye contact.

"Yeah nigga, dis the night I rock your world. Dis the one right here baby." He said as he rolled the dice up against the wall. "Head crack baby." He yelled as the dice showed 1 2 3.

Dontay pulled Supreme aside and told him that the guy rolling the dice is the same guy that Blue got into the shootout with.

"You sure?" Supreme asked then looked back at the guy on the dice.

"I'm positive! I never forget a face of an enemy, and any enemy of Blue's is an enemy of mines."

"Watch out!" He told Supreme as he pulled the .38 from the waist band of his pants, and before anyone knew what happened, a single shot put Blue's enemy brains on the pavement next to the dice.

"Oh Shit!" One of the dudes in the crap game jumped back and said.

"Come on!" Supreme said as he grabbed Dontay by the arm and led the way as they took off running. They ran as fast as they could through the projects, dipping in and out of building after building. Then ran up to the roof, then down the fire escape and through one of Supreme's girlfriend's bedroom window. They stayed there until the morning.

Blue got the word about what happened the next morning from Supreme. He immediately went to pick Dontay up and get him on the first thing smoking outta the city and back to DC.

"What up Kid? I heard you had one hell of a night last night." Blue said with a grin on his face more so happy that his enemy is now stiff as a board than the fact that Dontay was the one that made him that way.

"Yeah, something like that. Any enemy of yours is an enemy of mines and he had to be dealt wit."Blue looked over at Dontay as he drove towards the Brooklyn Bridge. "I gotta get you back to DC before someone find out you here with me, and have us both in Rikers, but first I got someone I want you to meet.

They drove across the Brooklyn Bridge on to FDR, then exited on 125th in Harlem.

Within minutes, they pulled up in front of an apartment building in Spanish Harlem where a young Puerto Rican kid name Julio had the hood on lock.

As they approached the building, Dontay's eyes lit up with excitement at the sight of the two salaciously dressed, curvaceous women that occupied the stoop; flirting with any and every man that walked by.

Blue noticed the look in Dontay's eyes, and smiled "Come on, you can't handle all that."

"You like doubting me huh? Didn't I prove you wrong about me the first time?"

Blue laughed "You gotta always bring your A-game with me if you want me to be a believer."

As they entered the building, although Blue was playing with his doubtful words, Dontay wasn't feeling the fact that it was the second time Blue had doubted him. He turned around to get another look at the girl in the pink spandex pants and thought to his self... **"Shid! He got me fucked up! Give me one chance and I'll fuck her brains out."**

As they made their way down the graffiti painted hallway, the girl on the stoop radioed in on her walkie talkie to alert her boss that two were on their way down the hallway.

Blue and Dontay stopped in front of apartment 1C and Blue gave a hard 7 code knock on the door. It was quickly opened by a short stubby older lady that had to be in her early 50's.

Blue addressed the lady as Momma Maria.

"Hola Hijo. Long time no see..." she said and gave him a hug.

"Who's this handsome young man?" She said referring to Dontay.

"This my Lil Brother Dontay"

"Hola Dontay. Nice to meet you. Welcome to my humble abode. Julio is in the back. Make yourselves at home. Mi casa es su casa." She said with a wide smile revealing perfect straight white teeth.

"Wait right here." Blue said, then walked down the tiny hallway towards the bedroom. The closer he got to the bedroom, the louder the sound of the money counter got. That sound only meant one thing to Blue... 'Life was good!'

"Yo! What up my dude?" Blue said at the sight of Julio wrapping rubber bands around stacks of money. Julio was a young baby faced Puerto Rican kid from the Boogie Down with the flyness and hustle of a Harlem nigga, but the ruggedness and griminess of a Brooklyn nigga.

"Yo! What's good playboy? They must've ran you up outta DC if you standing back in front of me so soon."

"Nigga I'm from Brooklyn. I don't get ran up outta nowhere. I run niggas outta there own city."

"O.K. baby, I here you Papi. What's the word?"

"I got someone I want you to meet."

Dontay was standing in the middle of the living room staring at a picture on the mantle place that caught his attention and looked real familiar. His memory of where he saw that picture gave him flashbacks of when he got into trouble for knocking over that exact same picture off his grandmother's dresser when he was a kid.

Juilo peeped through the beaded vertical blinds that separated his bedroom from the living room, then looked back at Blue with an unsure look on his face.

"That's your prodigy huh?"

"Trust me son, he the one! The projects we need to get into is a real gold mine. I'm talkin' bout a 20 keys a week type of gold mine, but we need to feed him in order to make that happen."

"You trust him?"... Julio asked.

"I wouldn't have brought him here if I didn't. Remember Fingers?"

"Julio's facial expression changed in a split second at the mere mention of the name. "Yeah, I remember that muthafucka! Why?"

Blue nodded his head in Dontay's direction... "His work!"

Julio turned his attention away from Blue and looked at Dontay through the blinds and shook his head in agreement. "O.K., Imma do this for you because I trust your judgment, but if something goes wrong, it's on you Papi."

Blue stepped from behind the blinds and the clattering sound of the beads caused Dontay to turn around. Before he could say a word, Julio stepped from behind the blinds carrying a black duffle bag and dropped it on the floor by Blue's feet... "Recuerda, está en ti." (Remember, it's on you.) He said and without saying a word to Dontay, he turned on his heels and disappeared behind the beaded blinds. Dontay stared at Julio for a moment and instantly felt the hatred reeking off Julio like some cheap cologne. There was a natural dislike for one another without ever saying a word to each other. Julio was Puerto Rican and Dontay was half Dominican.

"I hate them damn blinds." Blue said as he picked up the duffle bag and threw it over his shoulders. "You ready to get to work?" He turned towards Dontay and asked.

"I'm born ready." He replied.

After the brief encounter with Julio and Blue, Dontay drove to 42nd& 8th Avenue in Mid-Town

Manhattan. Blue put Dontay on the first Greyhound out of the city back to DC with 5 keys of coke at 18 grand per unit.

With his first murder under his belt and 5 bricks in the bag in the seat next to him, he felt as though he was more than ready to secure his place in the streets of DC. He glanced over at the bag on the seat next to him and thought about what Blue asked him back at Julio's apartment… **"Am I ready! Shid! I'mma show him how ready I am."** He said to himself with a smirk on his face as he placed his hand on the bag and looked out the window contemplating his next move like he was in a serious game of chess for his life.

DC OR NOTHING

"A teacher affects eternity; he can never tell where his influences may lead." -SB

He arrived back in DC a few hours later and didn't waste any time getting straight to business. He assembled his team of young hustlers at Ronetta's house and broke down the 5 keys into ounces, giving him a total of 180 ounces. Then as the sun began to set, they broke down ounce after ounce into $20 rocks and went hand to hand day in and day out. They were on one serious grind and customers were coming like clockwork. They pumped long and hard around the clock, stacking dollar on top of dollar until they got rid of every single crumb, pulling in over $300,000.

After giving Blue his $90,000, he gave his team $20,000 a piece and put the remaining $195,000 in his stash. As long as Blue was willing to front him the work on consignment, he would never tell Blue exactly how much they made off the block. Things were working out fine and Blue and Dontay was getting a lot of paper together until things started to slow and Blue's trips to DC became few and far between. The 20 bricks Julio was giving Blue dwindled to just 10... then from 10 to 5... then from 5 to none. Julio was fuckin up bad and it showed. The drought put him back to square one while Blue scrambled around for a new connect.

Some time had passed since Dontay's trip to New York and his life took a serious detour from his original course of action when Marquise approached him and told him that AL just got stabbed in the hallway of the apartment building by a crack head robber. Without any hesitation, Dontay took off running towards the back of the projects to aid his friend. He entered the building and ran to the side of the motionless body on the floor lying in a puddle of blood. He kneeled down and pulled the knife out of his neck then rolled the body over.

"What the fuck?!" He said as he jumped back when he noticed the face on the dead man wasn't the face of his friend.

Nosey tenants of the building began to peep their heads out their doors, to see what was going on in the hallway. They slammed their doors shut when they saw Dontay kneeling over top of the dead body with a knife in his hand.

The sound of police sirens filled the night air and got louder and louder the closer they got. Dontay stood up and walked away as calm as possible with the knife gripped tightly in his hand. He stepped out of the building to a crowd of spectators standing around with all their eyes glued on him.

The brightness of the flash light temporarily blinded him... "Freeze MuthaFucka! Don't you take another mutha fuckin' step or I'll blow your mutha fuckin' head off!" The fat over weight cop yelled as he pointed the gun and flashlight at Dontay's face.

Without any regard or respect for the cop's pistol pointing at his face, he turned on his heels and sprinted back inside the building and jumped down the entire flight of stairs and turned the corner of the building before the cop could react. He put enough distance between him and the fat cop making it impossible for him to catch him. He sprinted up the alley past a group of guys on the basketball court then down 14th street where he saw a friend from school name T-Mack leaning up against his apartment building counting his money.

Out of breath, he could barely talk but was able to convince T-Mack to let him hide out at his apartment until things died down. Then he could make his move to a safer location out of the city. The neighborhood was hotter than a whore's pussy with gonorrhea, on the Vegas strip in the middle of the summer; in 100 degree heat with corduroy pants on. Going to jail for something he didn't do wasn't conducive to his future.

The ghetto bird flew overhead for over an hour patrolling the hood by air. The police were on foot and in patrol cars combing through the entire neighborhood, looking for who they thought was the killer.

Dontay parlayed at T-Mack's well into the middle of the night and left when C.C. came to pick him up in his Cadillac Fleetwood. They pulled up at the Super 8 hotel in College Park, Maryland where he would lay low for the time being.

"You gonna be alright out here?" C.C. asked.

"Yeah, I'll be cool for now. Imma call the chick Brandy to come keep me company until I can find out what's up and why the fuck this nigga Marquise lied to me. Keep your ears to the streets and let me know if you hear anything."

"Say no more, I'm on it. Take this in case you need it." C.C. said and handed him a Taurus 9 mm and 2 grand. "Call me if you need me." C.C. turned and exited the room closing the door behind himself. Dontay put the gun underneath the pillow, and the money on the nightstand. He picked up the phone and called Brandy to come spend a little time with him, then got in the shower.

Brandy arrived at the hotel an hour later. She was looking sexy as usual in her pink silk blouse and pink linen pants, silk pink and turquoise scarf. She accessorized with a belt tied around her

CHAPTER

TEN

BACK ON THE BLOCK

"You don't have to go to college to get a degree in Criminal Street Law on how to survive."-SB

After 2 weeks of being stuck in the hotel with Brandy, she was starting to drive him crazy and he grew tired of fucking her all day, every day. He had to get back to business, and bring their rendezvous to an end ASAP. He needed to hit the streets and see what the word was about that body in the hallway.

C.C. arrived to pick them up and drove them to drop Brandy off at her mother's house on the Northeast side of DC.

"Look here slim, Dig this. I really think you should lay low and let me beat these streets and clean up this situation before you show your face out here. Word has it that the fiend Day-Day is the one with diarrhea of the mouth so I'm all over that, you dig? Oh yeah, before I forget"... C.C. paused and reached in his back pocket and pulled out a folded up piece of paper and handed it to Dontay. "Your man Rocko just came home. He told me to give you his number.

Dontay stared at the number for a second, and then put it in his pocket. C.C. glanced over at Dontay in the passenger's seat and stopped the car at a red light.

"Look, I'm on top of this situation and Imma make sure this shit never comes back to bite you in the ass. In the meantime, you need to stay off these streets. It's a Pernell Whitaker fight up Atlantic City tonight. You wanna go?"

Dontay had never been one to wait around for anyone else to do what he could do his self. He sat back in the passenger's seat and contemplated C.C.'s suggestion. He didn't want to put his- self in a vulnerable position without knowing what was being said about the body in the hallway, so he agreed to go to the fight in Atlantic City. They arrived in Jersey 30 minutes before the fight started and walked the board walk to see which players from the city came out for the event, and which chick was there looking for a come up. While they walked, enjoying the night air and the cool breeze that came off the ocean, a familiar face caught Dontay's attention. He walked over to say hello and approached the small group of men standing in front of the Ceaser's Palace Hotel and Casino.

"What's up my man? Remember me?" Dontay asked.

"Yeah, I remember you. You Blue's guy from DC right? I heard you doing some major numbers up the in the city." Julio said trying not to expose the fact that the keys Dontay was selling were actually his and not Blue's, but little did he know Dontay already knew what the meeting at his apartment was all about and he knew that Julio was now a full fledge coke head still trying to pass himself off as the man. Dontay was playing his own game of chess. He used them just as much as they thought they were using him. As long as they fronted him the coke on consignment for 18 grand a key and he was able to pocket a 54 grand profit; and as long as he never revealed to them that he spoke Spanish, he was winning all the way around.

He noticed the guy Julio was with had an unusual style that would've easily identified him as a certified bamma in DC. The Jerri curl hair style said either Mid-West or West Coast, but what stood out the most was the diamond flooded presidential Rolex that dangled off his wrist. It was something different about him. He wasn't rugged like the New Yorkers. He was a little more polished. The iced out Rollie said money, but his gear screamed bamma. However, who wrote the rule and said bammaz don't get money? He turned and looked at Dontay when he overheard Julio say he was Blue's guy in DC.

"You from DC huh? The guy with the Jerri curl asked and he could tell right away from his accent, that he definitely wasn't from New York.

"Yeah, I'm from the city. Where you from?"

"I just moved here from L.A. My name Troy." He said as he extended his hand towards Dontay.

"My name Dontay. I got family in LA. Inglewood...Hoover Street by Crenshaw Boulevard?"

"What you know 'bout Hoover?"

"I told you I got family from there. A wild cousin name Bob. They call him Cadillac."

"Get the fuck outta here! That's my Mu'fuckin' nigga right there. That's your cuzzin'?"

Troy dialed the number on his Motorola cell phone and within seconds, had Bob on the phone.

The phone call was brief and at that moment. Troy looked at Dontay and told him that if he needed anything don't hesitate to ask. He gave him his number, turned on his heels and headed to the casino.

"Well whata'ya know. Ain't dis 'bout a bitch. It really is a small world. Congratulations kid, welcome to the family. Just make sure you stay outta my way." Julio said with a mixture of sarcasm and hatred in his voice. Dontay stood there and watched them disappear into the casino lobby. C.C. approached him with a curious look in his eyes and directed his attention on who Dontay's focus was beamed in on.

Never taking his eyes off Troy until he was completely out of view.

"You aiight?" C.C. asked.

"This could be it right here big boi. This could be the break we needed."

He looked over at C.C. and asked "You wit me?"

"Is a pig pork?"

They laughed then walked towards the hotel and enjoyed the fight. A few weeks passed since meeting Troy in Atlantic City and he finally decided to give him a call. Troy was more than ecstatic about having someone in the city who he considered family. Bob had stamped Dontay's legitimacy, and it was more than enough for Troy to accept him with open arms and a open heart.

Bob had asked Troy to look out for him as if Dontay was him, and that's exactly what he did. He explained the situation to Troy about the body in the hallway, and Troy did any and everything in his power to make sure Dontay had everything he needed to be comfortable and safe until he got that situation cleaned up.

He put him in a lavish, fully furnished penthouse apartment in Rosslyn, Virginia overlooking the Georgetown Waterfront Park. The white leather sofa and love seat in the living room and a white marble coffee table that sat on top of the plush area rug, served as the residing place for the large statue of an all black nude woman. The expensive painting that hung on the wall above the sofa, the sparkling chandelier that hung from the ceiling and the large television all showed that Troy had exquisite taste.

After he got settled in, they made frequent trips back and forth to Cali, and Troy showed Dontay both sides of L.A. The grimy side of the ghetto in Inglewood and the glitz and glamorous side of the rich and famous of Hollywood.

A mild and inconsistent breeze soothed the night as Troy drove him all around in his black convertible 560 SEC Mercedes and introduced him to some of Cali's elite hustlers, as his little brother. They drove to Wilshire Boulevard between Sycamore and Fairfax Avenue to meet up with Troy's partner Head.

Head and Troy talked briefly then drove to one of Head's houses in Palos Verdes, California that sat on a manicured 18 acres of land with palm trees that lined the drive way on both sides leading up to the roundabout at the entrance. The house was a thing of a beauty and Dontay couldn't believe his eyes.

"You take care of that situation back in DC, and one day you can be pulling up to something like this of your own." Troy looked over and said to Dontay when he noticed him admiring the landscape.

At that very moment, his mission was clear. Clean up all loose ends back home so he could one day obtain everything that Troy had exposed him to and more. His aspirations of becoming a millionaire became stronger, and being in this position with Troy is exactly where he needed to be in order to make those dreams his reality.

The first order of business was to get on top of that situation about the body in the hallway and find out who was trying to set him up. Shortly after his plane landed at Dulles airport from LAX, he made the call to get the players off the bench and get them ready for game time.

You hear people say all the time that they don't play the big I, little U game, as if we're all equalbut the truth of the matter is everyone just isn't on the same level, and there can only be one boss.

Everyone must play their position in order for things to click on all cylinders. Troy was the owner of this all star team of dynamite young hustlers, Dontay coached and Calvin, C.C., Dan, Lil Crip and Terry were the starting five that could run with the best of them. They all grew up together since they were kids, so Dontay already knew each individual's strengths and weaknesses.

Everything ran smooth while Dontay made all his moves in the darkness of the night to avoid anyone pinpointing his whereabouts, until he could find out what's the word in the hood about the body in the hallway.

His crew grinded a lot of long nights, and it was beginning to take its toll on them. They wanted to take a break from the block so they all took a weekend trip to Cancun, Mexico and another trip the next weekend to the Aspen, Colorado ski resort.

Ever since he met Troy the money was coming in buckets at a time. Dontay moved Kilo after Kilo for Troy and could've easily monopolized the block, but decided the best way to keep jealousy and envy from eating at the hearts of men was to show them love and play fair with all those around him that were worthy of that kind of recognition.

A word of wisdom that his father told him was to never be selfish. If you take care of the hood, the hood will take care of you.

He employed the same man that started him off in the game with just 5 halves and fronted Kool 2 bricks at the same price Troy charged him. He felt it was only right to show him that kind of love since it was Kool's coke that he tossed the night he got locked up that jump started his passion for the hustle.

As the money piled up, so did the hate. Old timers who couldn't sell their product when Dontay and his crew came out on the block sucked on their teeth and sighed in exasperation at the mere sight of them, but they knew to stay quiet. Little did he know, the hate was about to come his way, brewed in the hearts of an entirely different beast that couldn't be contained so easily.

CHAPTER ELEVEN

IGNOMINIOUS BASTARD

"That which deceives us and does us harm, also undeceives us and does us good." – Joseph Roux

---

"Redman and Black get your asses in my office right now!" Captain Mark Torres of the 5th

District police precinct yelled out of the door way of his office.

"Shit!" Detective Black said as she looked over at her partner. Then got up from their desks and made their way to the captain's office not knowing what would be their fate.

"Close the door!" Captain Torres said in an agitated tone as he sat at his desk.

Detective Redman attempted to take a seat but was stopped in mid squat.

"Keep Standing!" The captain ordered as he lit his cigar. Then sat back in his recliner office chair and took a puff of his cigar then blew the smoke into the air.

"What the hell am I paying you for? Why the hell don't I have them Montana boys in my holding cell? I thought you told me that you had a witness to that murder in the hallway?"

"I don't know what happened Cap. The District Attorney

won't issue a warrant because the witness keeps giving conflicting statements about what he saw and no one else is saying a word." Detective Black said.

"We're beating the streets up as hard as we can Cap. No one is talking." Detective Redman chimed in.

"What you mean no one is talking? It's always someone willing to talk. Maybe y'all not asking the right questions or maybe you need to stop beating the streets up and start beating some heads up out there. I need an arrest on this case, and I need it ASAP.

"I got a surveillance team set up on the Terrace right now as we speak." Detective Redman said, in an attempt to ease the Captain's tension.

"Alright, let me know what, if anything turns up, because I got 9 unsolved homicides with Beltre's name attached to all of them, and you haven't seemed to be able to bring him in on even one."

"We're on it Cap." Detective Black said as they exited the office.

"Cap is right Black." Detective Redman turned and said as he and his partner walked out of the precinct. "We gotta get out there and start whopping some ass. Gotta start smacking some heads around and make these sons of bitches talk.

"Maybe we can be a little more aggressive with our interrogating, but I'm not with the brutal force tactic."

"LOOK! WHO'S SIDE ARE YOU ON!? What else can we do out here if these sons of bitches not giving us what we want. These cases not gonna solve their selves.

"Don't ever question what side I'm on. You can do what you want but I'm just not into smacking people around." Detective Black retorted as she got into the car.

They rode to Montana Terrace and parked on 14th street where they sat and watched the activity going on across the street by the clothes line through their binoculars. Their eyes were set on Rocko as he engaged in a conversation with another young hustler from the hood. Their view was obscured when the white Porsche 911 pulled up. Detective Redman moved the binoculars from his eyes as if he could see better without them, then put them back into use. He noticed Rocko walking towards the side of the building and retrieved a large shopping bag, then walked towards the Porsche and briefly exchange words with the driver before getting in on the passenger's side. Within a matter of seconds, Rocko was exiting the Porsche. Detective Redman turned the key in the ignition and got in pursuit of the Porsche. Following him turn for turn waiting for a legal reason to pull him over. He gave him none and Detective Redman's patience quickly ran out. "Fuck it!" He said as he turned on his lights and siren. They pulled the Porsche over on New York

Avenue. The detectives exited their car and approached the Porsche with their guns drawn.

"Driver, let me see your hands." Detective Redman ordered as he approached the car with caution. "License and registration! Did you not see that stop sign back there?" Detective Redman asked, but lied.

"No sir, I didn't see a stop sign."

Detective Redman looked at the driver's license… "Pierre Carter."

"Step outta the vehicle Mr. Carter!" Detective Redman ordered as he reached for the door handle and opened the driver's door.

"Put your hand on the hood and spread 'em." Detective Redman began to search him. Where you coming from Mr. Carter?" He asked.

"My girlfriend's house."

"Your girlfriend's house huh? Is your girlfriend name Rocko?"

"Huh?!"

"You heard what the fuck I said. Your girlfriend's name must be Rocko cause I just seen you pull up on 14th street, and Rocko got in and out of your car in a matter of seconds. So you wanna tell me the truth or do I gotta beat the truth outta you?"

Detective Black stood her ground and watched as her partner attempted to persuade Pierre to give him whatever information he had on Rocko and the Montana boys, by any means necessary.

"Search the vehicle!" He ordered his partner.

"You got any weapons or drugs in the car sir?" Detective Black asked.

Pierre remained silent while detective Black searched the vehicle. Detective Redman continued treating him with acts of violence if he didn't tell him something.

"Bingo!" Detective Black said as she held up an Adidas gym bag containing 3 kilos of cocaine.

"Isn't that the same gym bag we saw Rocko get into this car with?" Detective Redman asked his partner.

"It sure is."

"Well, well, well, looks like you gonna be going away for a very long time if you don't tell me where you got that coke from.

"I want a lawyer!"

"Listen here you little piece of shit!"Detective Redman slammed the man's head down on the hood of the car "If you don't tell me where the fuck you got that coke from, you gonna need more than a lawyer. Now where the fuck did...??? "DETECTIVE!" His partner yelled out in an attempt to stop him before he crossed the line. Just when he was about to put a foot up Pierre's ass, a passing by patrol car pulled over to back up their fellow officers.

After going through the formalities with the other officers now on the scene, they read Pierre his rights, booked him and took him to 5th District Station.

"Who is this?" The Captain asked upon their arrival at the station.

"We went to Montana Terrace to put a little pressure on the witness, and saw this individual pull up and Rocko get in and out of his vehicle. We pulled him over and conducted a search of the vehicle and found this, 3 kilos of cocaine." Detective Redman said handing the gym back over to the Captain.

"3 Keys huh?"...The Captain said as he looked inside of the gym bag, pulled out one of the kilos that was wrapped in black electrical tape, then looked at Pierre "What's your name?"

"Pierre Carter." He responded.

The Captain quickly picked up on the accent. "Where you from Pierre Carter?"

"Panama."

"You're a long way from home ain't you Pierre? What you doing up Montana Terrace with 3 kilos of coke?"

Pierre refused to answer.

"Looks like you're in deep shit right now Mr. Pierre. Did you get that coke from Rocko?"

Pierre still refused to answer. "O.K. suit yourself. You wanna play hard ball. Let's play hard ball.

Run his prints then contact DHS to start the process to get this son of a bitch deported back to

Panama." The Captain spit out then looked over at Pierre who was handcuffed to the bench.

"Give us a minute." The Captain turned to his detective and asked. Without a second thought, they exited the holding cell.

"Listen, it's not you that I want. I can make this whole thing go away if you just tell me that it was Rocko and Dontay that gave this to you. If not, then you can roll the dice and take your chances in court but I'm telling you, with 3 keys of coke, you'll be over District Court. That's federal if you didn't know, and if convicted, you're looking at something like 20 on the low end and maybe even deportation and I know you don't wanna do 20 years then get deported after. So help yourself by helping me, and this little 3 keys will disappear. I'mma give you a minute to think about it." The captain grabbed the gym bag, got up and left the holding cell.

"Redman, Black, my office!" The captain ordered.

"What's up Cap?" Redman asked as him and his partner entered the office.

"I sure hope you had probable cause to pull him over, cause any good attorney will destroy you at the arraignment. Take this and put it into evidence for now. He said and handed Redman the gym bag. In the meantime, I need you two to interrogate this asshole and see if you can get him to say Rocko or Beltre' gave him that coke. He's probably in there sweating bullets right now thinking about getting deported if he's convicted."

"I'm on it Cap." Redman said as he looked at his partner and exited the office.

"Grab a folder off your desk and follow me." Detective Redman told his partner while he put the gym bag containing the 3 kilos into his desk drawer. She was puzzled as to what he had in mind, but did as he asked.

"Well, well, well Mr. Carter. Looks like you're in deep shit this time my man." He reached for the folder from his partner, opened it and pretended to start reading. "You got an outstanding warrant for your arrest on top of a new charge for 3 kilograms of pure cocaine. UHM! That sounds like it's a rap for you my man. What that sound like to you Detective?" He turned and asked his partner.

"That sounds like someone gonna be spending a lot of time thinking about that opportunity to help yourself, that you let get away from you on your way back to Panama."

Pierre sat back up against the wall, exhaled and dropped his head.

CHAPTER

TWELVE

YOU CAN RUN BUT YOU CAN'T HIDE

"A time will come when a snake will reveal his self." – SB

A month has passed since Pierre's arrest. It was New Year's Eve and the Metro Club was like that on Thursday nights. All the players & all the honey's from around the surrounding areas from Montana, 18th & D, Brentwood, The Arboretum, Fort Lincoln, Ivy City, Trinidad, the Hechinger Mall Honey's, Sursum Corda, First Street, Le'Droit Park, Rosedale, Benning Road, Simple City, Barry Farms, Valley Green, Congress Park, Woodland all the way to Largo, Landover, and Capital Heights, Maryland. All the hustlers and the fly honeys came to the Metro Club on Thursday nights to party. Dontay made a grand entrance and all eyes were on him.

The D-Jay was playing Slick Rick's "Hey Young World" when he walked in and shouted out his name.

Always smooth, charismatic and confident, his presence always demanded attention. He was that nigga that the bitches wanted to be with and the bitch niggaz wanted to be like. Although he's not the drinking type, he made sure that everyone around him had a good time. He bought 48 bottles of Moet just to pour the ladies drinks. He caught Marquise mean mugging him from afar but Dontay didn't allow himself to become rattled and he kept his composure and shrugged it off with a smile but, he wanted to agitate Marquise just enough to fuck up his night with a touch of arrogance to let him know who the jefe is. Dontay made his way to where Marquise was standing up and placed his arm around Marquise neck.

"What's up playboy? What's wrong with your face?" Dontay asked, but received no reply from an irritated Marquise who remained silent and became agitated in his own right at Dontay's approach. He hated the fact that Dontay was now in position and moving up fast, and that he was stuck selling halves for Kool, who was getting his work from Dontay. So in all actuality, Marquise ended up working for Dontay anyway and he hated it.

"Check this out slim! If you wouldn't let your bummy pride get the best of you, you would be a part of all this. I remembered what you said about me being a pawn for the New Yorkers, but you can never underestimate the power of a pawn that maneuvers on the board the right way. Never forget that a pawn can grow up to be the strongest piece in the game. That's one to grow on champ! Here you go, take this bottle of Mo, put down that Heineken, fix your face and stop looking so uptight and get you one of these bitches up in here. Enjoy your night. Oh yeah, before I forget, tell your boss Imma need my money by tomorrow."

Dontay stepped off, and motioned a pretty brown skinned female to accompany Marquise up against the wall. His arrogance only infuriated Marquise's hatred for him even more, but Marquise was the least of his worries.

He maneuvered his way through the crowd towards the restroom when he saw Blue and Julio huddled up by the arcade machine talking to Rocko. He hadn't seen Blue in a while, and wanted to welcome him and Julio to the city with open arms and roll out the red carpet for them; now that he was in that boss position to do so. The hypnotic rhythm of that plan came to a screeching halt, and his night became a little more interesting when he noticed a familiar face on the dance floor.

Music was blasting out of the speakers and people were dancing, laughing, congregating, networking and having a good time all around him but Dontay's focus was zeroed in on something entirely different. C.C. was surrounded by a group of beautiful women when Dontay approached him and gave him a head nod towards the dance floor and in true C.C. fashion without a moment's hesitation, he sat his drink on the table and shadowed Dontay's every step. C.C. quickly noticed what Dontay's eyes were focused on.

C.C. looked at Dontay with an enraged look in his eyes "What you wanna do?" Without another word from Dontay's mouth they made their way through the crowd towards the exit.

Once outside they walked to the car, C.C. got a shot gun with a pistol grip, handed it to Dontay along with a black Champion hoody, black gloves and a Freddie Kruger Halloween mask.

"Keep the car running, I won't be long." Dontay said as he pulled the mask down over his face and squatted down between the parked cars. Day-Day walked out of the club staggering in his walk from having a little too much to drink. Not knowing who or what was lurking in the darkness waiting for him. It appears that he's walking directly towards where his worst nightmare awaits him.

"Come on muthafucka." Dontay said anxiously. Day-Day took 4 more steps and Dontay couldn't wait any longer. He raised up from behind the car and pointed the shotgun center mass at his chest...

BOOM! The first blast from the shot gun caused Day-Day's body to hit the pavement fast and hard. He struggled for air as he began to gag on his own blood. Dontay stood over top of him and pumped 3 more shots into Day-Day's face and body. He made his getaway as smooth as possible and made it back to the car where C.C. waited. C.C. broke the shot gun down and disposed of it piece by piece into a sewer. Dontay took off the hoody, mask and gloves and torched them.

Police sirens were coming from everywhere but C.C. remained calm as he drove off. They made it back to Montana Housing Projects where C.C. pulled up alongside Dontay's car. Before exiting the car, he sat there in silence for a moment reflecting on what Troy told him about cleaning up his situation and things would open up for him in a major way.

"You good?" C.C. asked.

"Yeah, yeah I'm good. I'll see you in the a.m." He said as he got out the car.

C.C. watched with a concerned look on his face as his best friend walked away.

CHAPTER
THIRTEEN

SYMPOSIUM AT HOUSTON'S

"A leader is best when people barely know that he exists, not so good when people obey and acclaim him, worst when they despise him."

-Lao Tzu

Later that evening, he met with his crew at the clothes line on 15th Street when Detective Redman and Detective Black rode by real slow and just stared at them. They were taking their usual mental photographs of them.

"Them mutha fuckaz is up to something slim, that's the second time today these mu'fuckaz rode pass here." C.C. said.

Once the Taurus was out of sight, they all dispersed and met up at Houston's restaurant in Georgetown. Dontay didn't want to play the big "I" and the little "U" thing with his crew but, he quickly noticed them getting lazy once they bought dirt bikes and cars, and had countless bitches to fuck. He noticed them getting a little too comfortable and complacent with what they had acquired so far. Dontay wasn't satisfied. He wanted the long term riches, not just a few hundred thousand. He wanted to be wealthy and his crew was beginning to lose that drive and hunger. After his conversation with Troy, Dontay figured this was the perfect time to discuss his displeasure as to the direction his crew was headed in and to prepare them for what's to come.

"Dig this!" He said, then paused and waited until he had their attention before he proceeded on. "I don't know if you niggaz is content with the little bit of paper we got right now or what, but I'm not! I noticed that nobody wanna hustle no more. Y'all niggaz think y'all bosses now huh? All you niggaz wanna do is ride around all fucking day doing nothing and going nowhere, and ain't making no money. How much you get off the block today?" Dontay said as he turned his attention to Lil Crip.

"I ain't even been there today." Lil Crip responded.

"How much you get Terry?"

"I ain't make nothing." Terry answered.

"My point exactly! That's the shit I'm talkin' bout right there. You niggaz is getting lazy. I remember the old heads used to call us "Hustle Boys" because we would fall asleep some nights from being out there on the grind all mutha fuckin night. Now look what's happening to us, we getting lazy, too big headed, or both. We need to tighten up and get back on our shit before they start calling you niggaz "Nothing Boys" because that's exactly what the fuck you niggaz gonna have if that's all you niggaz wanna do is ride around all damn day. NOTHING!"

Dontay wasn't just the strength of the crew, he was also sagacious and mentally keen about the streets, the business side of the hustle, and all the rules to it. He was well ahead of his time from all the schooling he had been exposed to at an early age by all the older dudes he had as teachers. He knew he had to step up, and put order and control back into his crew because they were getting out of control with their spending and starting to get too damn lazy.

"I wanna ask you niggaz a question, and if any one of y'all can answer it, I won't say another word about this shit ever again. And, I'll let you niggaz do what yall wanna do because maybe y'all know something that I don't know, but answer me this... "Name one business, JUST ONE where everybody in that business is the boss? He asked the question knowing that no one would be able to answer it. He looked around the table to see who would have the gull to even try.

"NOT ONE! Businesses don't operate that way, and what we're running is a business. Let's not lose focus of that. This is NOT A GAME!" He expressed with emphasis. "The moment you approach this business like it's a game; you already lost. Everyone has a position to play, and the business we're in is no different. I love you niggaz like brothers and I want all of y'all to eat out here like you're supposed to. I mean, really eat! But you niggaz not taking this business serious enough. We're in a different position than a lot of these niggaz out here, and we can't fuck this up. I want us all to be able to retire from this shit wealthy men one day, but in order for that to happen, you niggaz gotta start playing your positions. Is y'all in or out?" Dontay took a sip of his orange juice and looked around the table. Terry responded…"You're right slim. It's time we park these mutha fuckin' cars and get back to work. My pockets been hurtin' for real… Shit ain't been the same since I got that mutha fuckin car."

Dontay looked at Lil Crip with a look of disappointment in his eyes, and Lil Crip knew the whole speech was directed at him because ever since they were kids, Lil Crip has always been one of the crew's best hustlers. He really would be the first mutha fucka on the block for the cheese, and the last mutha fucka to leave.

"Imma need everyone to step it up 10 notches and get back to business because things are going to get real serious, real quick and Imma need everyone of y'all to start operating with a little more tenacity and motivation. I want a better life for us all after this, but first we got money to get. So, let's toast to the hustle and a successful life after the hustle." They all raised their glasses "To the Hustle" Dontay said. "To the Hustle"… they all repeated.

"Hustle Boys" were back on the grind. They were hungry again. They got back to work and made $216,000 off the 3 bricks they broke down and grabbed another $14,000 off the other 1 brick that he broke down into 8th's... bringing in $230,000. They repeated the process and got rid of 4 of the 10 keys that Rocko was supposed to sell to Pierre. He gave Troy the $180,000 he owed him for the 10 keys and divided up the other $280,000 between the 5 of them...giving them $55,000 a piece. Dontay was now sitting on a hefty $563,000 of his own cash. And well on his way to reaching his goal of becoming the millionaire he always dreamed of being and with the new position Troy was about to put him in, he was sure to solidify his place at the round table of bosses amongst the city's elite in no time.

Things were moving faster than expected, and the bigger his operation grew, the more complex things became. He embraced all that came with this level of the business, the fakeness, the crude, the envy, the hate, the 50 playing, the snitching, the murders. He embraced it all, and he refused to leave caution in the wind. He invested in heavy artillery and hired drivers with fake law enforcement credentials to transport the work up and down the beltway, but at times things became a little overwhelming and he just wanted to take a break from it all to clear his mind and just relax for a minute; and feel a sense of normalcy again.

He drove to Hains Point and walked the strip. He smiled at the sight of families picnicking, enjoying their time together. Couples hugging and kissing up against their cars, walking the strip hand and hand, and laid out on their picnic blankets feeding each other strawberries and sipping on their wine when he noticed a female sitting alone on her blanket reading a novel and sucking on a blow pop. He stopped and stared at her for a moment, admiring her natural beauty and how her hair hung down to the middle of her back.

"Is it good?" He asked when he approached her.

She glanced up at him, then directed her attention back to her book "It's alright, but I like part one better."

"I was talkin' bout that blow-pop. I can tell you were really into that book because you was tearing that joint up. He tried to pull a smile out of her but got a menacing stare instead.

"Are you waiting for someone?"

"No, I'm not waiting for anyone but I'm really trying to read my book if you don't mind."

He squatted down beside her "What's your name?" He asked.

"Stacy" she answered with a sigh of slight irritation.

"Nice to meet you Stacy, I'm Dontay." As he extended his hand.

"Can I sit with you and keep you company for a minute?"

Before she could decline, he claimed his seat beside her. They talked for over an hour and hit it off pretty good. As hard as she tried not to give in, she couldn't resist his charm. They shared similar interests and goals in life and shared intimate stories about their childhood. They talked and laughed well into the middle of the night.

It was getting late so they exchanged numbers and made plans to see each other again. He walked her to her car, opened the door and made sure she drove off safely. She smiled as she drove off at the thought of how easy she gave in to his charm.

CHAPTER

FOURTEEN

M.O.B.

Early the next morning, he got up and did his routine 1,000 sit ups and 1,000 pushups. Got in the shower, then made last minute preparations for his date with Stacy.

He made reservations at the Hogate's Restaurant in SW DC then made his way over to Stacy's. She came out wearing a pair of olive green Palmetto jeans, hugging her in all the right places. Her tan and green floral print silk top was accented by a pair of tan high heels, a brown leather MCM purse, and an Asymmetric hair style that had her looking as good as she did the day he met her.

"You look nice." He told her.

"Thank you, so do you.

They arrived at the restaurant a little after 9pm and was shown their seat by the window with the waterfront view, the décor was exquisite, and the quaint architecture enhanced the ambiance. The lighting was dim, but the small lamp that sat in the middle of the table between them illuminated their faces just enough for him to see the color of her eyes.

Hardly the drinking type, Dontay ordered a glass of orange juice for his self and Stacy ordered a pre-mixed batch cocktail and a shot of Remy Martin XO. For the main course, Dontay settled for a well done New York strip steak and Stacy had the lobster and chocolate mousse for desert.

They talked and laughed for well over two hours about life, family and where they saw themselves in the next 5 years. Stacy was on her third year in medical school and expressed interest in one day getting married and having a big family. Her temperament was sensitive and innocent, so he tried not to display any signs of ruggedness that would send her running for the hills and he prayed to God that no one from the underworld came in and exposed his hand. He really liked her because she was different. She was smart and wanted to do something constructive with her life. Dontay on the other hand, was the complete opposite. He didn't want to get married and he didn't want a lot of children. His life was more on the destructive road, but to him, he had it all under control. He shared with her a part of his life that he never felt comfortable with talking about, and told her how he witnessed his father getting gunned down right in front of him when he was 11. She felt compassion for him and seen the hurt in his eyes when he spoke of his dad.

She really liked him and enjoyed every minute of his company, and it was refreshing that she had finally found someone that was into her and wasn't into the street life. Finding a young black man on the streets of Washington DC., during a time when The Nation's Capital was dubbed the **"Murder Capital,"** was like finding a needle in a hay stack.

Just when things were going well, duty called. His pager started to vibrate and as bad as he wanted to ignore it, he couldn't. The motto Rocko once taught him was "You can never lose a bitch chasing paper, but you can lose paper chasing a bitch."

He looked down at his pager and noticed Rocko's code and 911. He excused his self and got up from the table and made his way to the phone booth in the lobby area. He dialed the digits as fast as his fingers could move, hoping that the distress code didn't come with any bad news.

"Hello!" Rocko answered.

"Yeah, what's wrong?"

"Where you at?" Rocko asked.

"I'm at Hogates. Why, what's wrong?"

"Duty calls my nigga. It's show time baby. P tryna get 10 tickets for tonight's show."

"Oh yeah??? Say no more. Meet me at the club house."… Click!

He hated to cut his date short with Stacy, but 10 joints meant 200 grand that he wasn't about to let no bitch stop him from getting, no matter how fine she was. "Fuck it! She just gotta be mad! My only obligation is to my men and getting this money." He said to his self as he made his way back to the table.

"Is everything o.k.?" She asked.

"Yeah, everything is good but something unexpected came up and I gotta go handle some real important business." By the look on her face, he could tell that she wasn't too happy about that. So, he promised her that he would make it up to her! He put his right hand over his heart as if that would make her believe him. Stacy was pissed, but went with the flow of things because if it really was as important as he said, she didn't want to seem insensitive.

"I understand, but you better make it up to me." She replied.

"I will." He said

He watched Stacy closely from behind as she walked towards the door and was instantly turned on by the way her ass jiggled and how soft it looked when it swayed from side to side.

"Damn! I can't wait to hit that ass from the back." He thought to himself.

Within minutes he pulled up in front of Stacy's house. Her dad was sitting on the front porch and sat up when the car pulled up to get a good look at the occupants inside, only to see his daughter exit the passenger side.

After she and Dontay said their goodbyes for the evening, she made her way towards the house and her smile instantly turn to a frown at the sight of her dad sitting on the porch.

"Who the hell is that dropping you off in a Mercedes?"

"None of your business. Dang daddy. Stop being so nosey."

"It's always my business as long as you living under my roof young lady. I hope you ain't out there in them streets messing with no hustler. I lost both of my parents to drugs, and I'll be damn if I'm gonna let my only daughter get mixed up in them streets with some drug dealer."

"He's not a drug dealer daddy." She retorted as she ran up the stairs to her bed room.

Her dad followed her into the house and stood at the bottom of the stairs and yelled up to her "Remember what I told you about these hustlers out here. They only gonna end up in one place or the other, jail or the grave!"

"BAM!"The sound of Stacy's door slamming shut ended the conversation.

Shortly after dropping Stacy off, Dontay got on the beltway and headed to his stash spot in a remote location in Maryland to pick up the 10 bricks. His pager vibrated non-stop.

"I'm coming nigga damn!"

He said to his self as he loaded up the Nike gym bag with the 10 bricks, and threw it over his shoulder, put on his black Banana Republic bucket hat, and pulled it down as low as it would go. He checked the clip in his 9mm Beretta, then cocked it to load a round in the chamber and walked out of the building looking side to side to make sure no unexpected guest showed up. He tossed the gym bag on the passenger's seat then got into the 1988 Pontiac Firebird and drove below the speed limit back to the city.

CHAPTER
FIFTEEN

EYES WIDE SHUT

"Sometimes the smallest mistakes carry the biggest consequences." —SB

Meanwhile... back in the city on the Northeast side of town. Detective Redman and Detective Black sat outside the Cloisters apartment complex waiting to capitalize on their informant's promise to hand deliver Dontay and Rocko on a silver platter with 10 keys of coke.

Detective Redman's patience was starting to wear thin, and his anxiety began to boil when the black Mercedes they were told to keep an eye out for never showed up. "GOT DAMN IT!" He said as he slammed his fist down hard on the dash board. "We been sitting here for over 3 fuckin' hours waiting on this son of a bitch."

"I thought the C.I. said he was on his way?"... Detective Black asked.

"He did. That was over 3 freakin' hours ago."

"You think the C.I. played us?" Detective Black asked.

Not wanting the thought of being made to look like a complete fool enters his thoughts, so he remained quiet and refused to give legs to Black's insinuation.

"Son of a bitch!" Detective Redman yelled out then loosened his tie and eyed every car that drove past. They sat for another hour before realizing that they been had.

"He's not showing up. That son of a bitch played us. I swear Black, Imma get these sons of bitches if my life depends on it."

Detective Black sat quiet as her partner rambled on and on about his desire to get the Montana boys by any means necessary. She noticed a change in him and heard the anger and the hate in his voice. He was becoming a different kind of animal, and she couldn't understand why he had such a hard on for Rocko and Dontay Beltre.

A little after 11pm, he arrived at what he called the club house because of its secured location where only crew members went to meet. Rocko was already there, and the closer he got to the door, the louder the sound of music grew.

"I know mu'fuckin' well this nigga ain't... It sound like a party up in this joint."

Dontay put his ear to the door and heard muffled voices over the loud music. He put his key in the door, unlocked it, and slowly opened it only to see a living room full of females partying and dancing like strippers.

"What the fuck is all this?!"

"Aw nigga never mind that, come on in the back." Dontay stared at Rocko, and could see that he was intoxicated, but off what was a question that couldn't be determined off first glance.

Dontay motioned with a head jester for Rocko to get up and follow him to the bed room down the hall.

"What the fuck is all this? He said surveying the room. "You got bitches all up in here and you twisted. Look at you. You can't even stand up straight! We never did business with bitches around. You slipping bad bruh. You need to tighten up! You gotta remember that the smallest mistakes sometimes carry the biggest consequences." Dontay said as he looked Rocko up and down, then turned on his heels and walked out the room.

"Aw nigga, I ain't drunk. I just had a little bit of champagne with these bad bitches up in here."

"I ain't doing this tonight slim. I'm out!"

"Hold up, hold up. What you mean you ain't doing this? He ready now."

"Naw nigga, YOU ain't ready. I'll see slim another day." Dontay rarely went against his first intuition. If he didn't feel comfortable with a situation, he bounced. Call it paranoid, he called it cautious.

CHAPTER SIXTEEN

DO YOU SMELL WHAT I SMELL?

"If the window of perception were cleansed; everything would appear to man as it is. Everything isn't always what it seems." –William Blake

Detective's Redman and Black walked back into the station frustrated and furious about the false lead and wild goose chase the C.I. sent them on. Detective Redman walked to his desk without saying a word and kicked his desk as hard as he could. "Son of a bitch!" He yelled. His desk drawer came open revealing the gym bag. He stared down at it for a moment then quickly closed it when his partner approached. "You want a cup of coffee?" She asked.

"Naw, thanks. I'mma go over a few more leads to see what we can come up with."

"Don't over work yourself Red. It'll come and when it does, it'll be the sweetest feeling." She said trying to relax her partner with reassuring words of encouragement, but he wasn't hearing any of that. His frustrations were over boiling, and he needed Dontay and Rocko as bad as a fish needed water. He took two anxiety pills, sat back in his chair and checked his messages. One was from his wife telling him not to forget to bring home milk, and the other was from his golf buddy John. The 3rd was from Pierre. His voice came through the speaker, which caused Detective Redman to receive mixed feelings. He was both happy and angry to hear from Pierre after coming up empty handed on his promise to deliver him the bust. He set up a meeting with Pierre outside of the city, where they hoped no one would see them.

While Detective Redman was gearing up for his meeting with Pierre, Dontay was headed to a meeting of his own with Stacy at her aunt's house in Fort Washington, Maryland. She was gorgeous to say the least and he couldn't stop thinking about those beautiful hazel eyes and her hour glass figure. Besides, it was only right that he made it up to her for the other day. He pulled up and noticed she was standing in the driveway waiting on him looking as sexy as she looked the first day he laid eyes on her. She got into the car where they sat and talked for over an hour and he fired off compliment after compliment of how sexy she looked and how he loved the soft melodic sound of her voice that was close to a seductive whisper when she talked. It was an exhilarating hour and the attraction between the two was magnetic and undeniably intense. Nothing could have prepared him for the degree of ecstasy he felt in her presence. The way she bit down on her bottom lip and looked at him was an invitation for him to kiss her. He leaned forward over the center console and kissed her passionately. Neither one of them could hold back the unbridled sexual desire that overwhelmed them at that very moment. He began to unbutton her blouse, when the bright lights of her aunt's car pulling in front of them deflated their moment.

For the first time he felt pure passion. He really liked Stacy, and he felt a bond building between them. He was always told to never put a bitch before business, but damn! What harm would it do to his business, showing a little love for? At that very moment, he could not think of anything else.

Although the threat of incarceration or death loomed over his head every single day of his life, he was more consumed with the streets and neglected to enjoy the simple pleasures that life had to offer until he met Stacy. Dontay was a real general to the hustle and he wasn't ready to allow his life to be overwhelmed by the beauty Stacy possessed. He just wasn't ready to relinquish that kind of control of his feelings to a woman and lose focus of his agenda. They continued to talk until the sun came up.

They drove to a nearby McDonald's for breakfast where he saw a couple of familiar faces that stood out like the Grand Wizard of the KKK in the middle of the Million Man March.

"What The fuck?!" He said as he drove into the parking lot. He reached for his gun but thought twice when he realized Stacy was in the passenger's seat next to him.

"What's wrong?" She asked.

"Nothing. Come on, we can't eat here! Don't ask me why but we gotta go."

Stacy was confused as to his sudden change in attitude and demeanor. This was the second time he had to abruptly leave because of some unexpected circumstance. He dropped her off back at her aunt's, hauled ass back to the city and got a room at the Embassy Suites Hotel on Military Road N.W.

He called his entire crew and told them to come see him right now.

"Get y'all asses up here right now." He ordered.

Pacing the floor in disbelief of what he saw; his mind was moving in a million different directions. A knock at the door broke his concentration. He pulled out his 9mm and looked through the peep hole. C.C., Lil Crip, and Travis all walked in together.

"What's good playboy? What's so important that this couldn't wait til later?"

"Later just might be too late!" He said as he continued to pace the floor rubbing his head and scratching his head. They all looked around at each other and were puzzled as to what was going on. They never have seen him like this.

"What's up slim? What' da fuck is up?" C.C. asked.

Another knock at the door broke the silence in the room. "It's JR and Terry." C.C. said as he opened the door to let them in. They dapped each other up then looked around the room with confused looks on their faces. Travis shrugged his shoulders when JR looked at him. Dontay still not saying a word pacing the floor contemplating his next move like a seasoned chess player before speaking. Dan and Pat arrived shortly after JR. and Terry. "Y'all seen Rocko?" He asked never breaking stride in his pacing.

"Naw, we ain't seen him all week." Pat answered.

"Page that nigga 911." He ordered. C.C. picked up the phone and dialed the digits.

Rocko was on the other side of town in Ivy City Northeast, laid up with one of his many jump offs. He grabbed his pager from off the night stand and saw the 911 with Dontay's code behind and tossed the pager on the floor. He was still harboring feelings about him not letting him bust that move with Pierre for the 10 bricks. "How the fuck he gonna do me like that?! Out of all people, ME!" Shid, I started this nigga off in this business and this how the fuck he treat me? Imma show this nigga. You ain't no boss nigga! I'm da mu'fuckin' BOSS! I started you off in this shit nigga. Fuck That!" Rocko angrily expressed to his female friend who was too high to give a fuck about anything he was talking about but agreed with him anyway.

"Yeah, you right baby. You da boss. Fuck that! Here, hit this." She said as she laid out a line of coke on the night stand.

Meanwhile, back at the hotel...Dontay finally stop pacing. "Aiight, dig this. I'll get with that nigga Rocko later. This shit is too serious to put off any longer. We got a serious problem on our hands that gotta be addressed ASAP. I just seen the nigga Pierre talking to Detective Redman at the McDonald's out Fort Washington. Rocko was suppose to hit him off with 10 of the joints yesterday, but I gated the move cause he was drunk as shit."

"So you think he was trying to bring slim a move?" JR. asked.

"Maybe, maybe not...but in this business, any dealers with the cops raises suspicions that can't be ignored. Look here Travis, Imma need you to get on top of this ASAP. Don't waste no time! I need this done like right now in order to keep all of us outta 1901 D. street."(DC Jail)

"Hold on D. You're not even sure if the nigga was telling on us or what he was talking to Redman about."

"Do you hear yourself nigga?! Do it matter what he was talking to Redman about? He shouldn't been talking to the law at 5 in the morning any fuckin' way. And even if he ain't talkin' bout us, so what! We might be saving somebody else from catching a case. Get on top of it and clean this nigga up."

"I'm just sayin."

"You just saying what?! Huh! What the fuck is you just saying? Cause right now I'm not understanding why the fuck you not getting it cause ain't NO PASSES GIVEN TO NO NIGGA that threatens our life and our freedom. PERIOD! Aye JR., holla at your weed man uptown and see if you can get a line on this rat bastard P."

"I'm on it slim."

"As a matter of fact, Imma role with you cause when you need something done and right, you gotta do it your got damn self." He said looking over at Travis, then exited the suite with JR., C.C. and Terry in tow.

CHAPTER SEVENTEEN

CHESS NOT CHECKERS

"Move the right pieces at the right time for conducive results." –SB

After the meeting at the Embassy Suites with the crew, Dontay and JR pulled up at the Blue Moon store on Georgia Ave, where JR's weed connect pumps ounces of chronic, incense, Bob Marley T-shirts, rings, necklaces, and hats. Basically whatever you wanted that was associated within the Rasta community, he sold it.

"JR, what's happening brethren?" He said in a distinctive Jamaican accent as we approached him.

"What's up Rude Boy?" JR returned the greeting with a hand shake and embraced him with a man hug.

"This is my man Dontay." JR said as he introduced the two men. Rude Boy extended his hand to Dontay and noticed the Rolex on Dontay's wrist.

"Respect Brethren." He said as he flashed his own Rollie. He handed JR a fat blunt of chronic, and JR didn't hesitate to fill his lungs with the intoxicating smoke.

"Here you go." JR said with a mouth full of smoke as he handed the blunt back to Rude Boy.

Rude boy grabbed the blunt and tried to pass it to Dontay "Nah, I don't smoke."

"You don't know whatcha missing. Dis right here, tis da best ting to ever come from da earth.

All natural "Gonja" straight from da all mighty "Jah" em self."Dontay gave JR the head nod to get to business.

"Aye, Rude Boy. Don't you know the boy Pierre?" JR asked.

Da Panamanian kid from New York? Yeah. Me know da kid. Me don't really get down wit 'em tho ya see. Da boy too sneaky for me brethren, he supposed to have whipped up a few birds but da shit came up short. Da kid went under da table on me ya see, so me don't trust 'em ya, see."

"My man right here know how to put that whip game down real proper and turn 1 brick into 1/ ½ easy." JR said as he head nodded towards Dontay. He just wanted to get to the business at hand. The last thing he wanted to do right about now was to discuss whip work but he went with the flow.

"Oh yeah! Dat's what me been lookin for. Somebody to blow some bricks up ya see. Come come, follow me." Rude Boy got up and they followed him to his room in the back of the store. They walked down a dim lit hall to the backroom. A tall slim Jamaican with thick dreadlocks that hung down past his waist, sitting in the dark room full of marijuana smoke listening to Bob Marley.

"Damn! That shit is strong as e mu'fucka." Dontay said as he tried to fan away the smoke in front of his face.

Rude Boy told his man who they were, and told them that Dontay knew how to put the come back on the yayo.

The Bob Marley wanna be didn't say a word. As he puffed on his blunt, looked at Dontay for a second, then leaned up and said in his Jamaican accent as he put his blunt in the ashtray.

So you know how to whip up work huh?

"Yeah, I can do a little something" Dontay said with a slight laugh.

"Show me!"

"I can show you but that kind of information comes with a price."

"Name it!"

Dontay really didn't want anything from Rude Boy. He would have shown him for free in exchange for the whereabouts of the rat Pierre, but since his man JR was a cold weed head, it was only right that he got him some of that shit for free.

"Give my man right here a couple of ounces of that weed you smoking.

"Dat's all?"

"Yeah, that's all." Dontay said.

Rude Boy yelled to his man "Get da boy a whole ting of dat good earth." He stood up and extended his hand out to him and said.

"Me name Javier."

Dontay shook his hand, then introduced himself.

Dontay and Javier left the store and went to a small apartment building down the block. JR stayed at the store with Rude Boy.

Dontay and Javier made small talk as they went into the building and up 2 flights of stairs to his apartment.

At first glance, Dontay was surprised to see that the joint was laid out but it smelled just like the room in the back of the store.

"Damn! All you do is smoke weed all day huh man?" Javier laughed, then walked to the bedroom.

He came back in less than 5 minutes with a small bag in his hand and dumped a bag of powder out of the top of the coffee table in the living room.

"Dat's an 8th. Can you blow dat up?" Javier asked.

"You got a microwave in here?"

"It's right there."

"You got some baking soda and some room deodorizer?"

"Yeah, hold on." He reached in the cabinet under the sink and handed him a clear glass bowl and a box of Armor Hammer Baking soda from the refrigerator.

"Here you go! What you gonna do wit dat?"

Dontay didn't respond verbally. He just looked at Javier and damn near sprayed the whole can in the air.

"Ha, ha, ha, ha" Javier laughed.

"I need more thing" Dontay said.

"What?" Javier replied.

"I need some Isotope."

"Some what?!" Javier asked,

"Isotope. That's what I put in the coke to blow it up." Dontay replied.

"Dat nigga Pierre didn't use that when he tried to do it for me."Javier said.

"That's because Pierre didn't know what the fuck he was doing." Dontay replied.

"Nah! I lost about a half a key fucking with dat nigga." He said as he sucked his teeth.

"Damn! How much was you trying to whip up?" Dontay asked.

"Tree bricks." Javier replied.

"If he would have put some Isotope on it, it would've blew up." Dontay knew Javier didn't have any Isotope when he asked him. He just threw it out there because he really wasn't there for that. He played along for as long as he had to in order to get the information on Pierre's whereabouts.

"I tink Pierre's girl dat lives upstairs might got some of dat stuff you talkin' bout because she be cooking too. What's the name if it again?"

"Isotope." Dontay said.

"Yeah, some of dat right there." Javier said with a smirk on his face.

"Pierre's girl lives upstairs?" Dontay asked.

"Yeah! Me really don't like da bitch. She too sneaky and nosey ya see but I'ma see if she got some of dat Iso stuff ya need. What's it called again?" Javier asked.

Dontay shook his head and laughed "Man! You really need to stop smoking that shit cause it's fucking your brain up."

Javier laughed "Me like you Brethren."

They got to the door of the apartment. Javier knocked on the door and a little girl about 10 years young in pigtails opened the door.

"Is ya mommy home pretty girl?" Javier asked.

The little girl just shook her head no... "My aunt Pam here." The little girl replied.

"Can you call you Auntee Pam for me?" Javier asked.

The little girl yelled out for her aunt "Aunt Pam, two mens want you at the door." The little girl shouted.

"What I tell you about opening that door!?" The tall slender woman said as she pulled the door open.

"What's up Javier?" Pam said as she looked Javier up and down with a serious grit.

"Let me holla at you for a minute" Javier said.

Pam stepped out into the hallway and slightly closed the door behind her.

"I know this girl" Dontay said to himself as he started flipping through his mental rolodex trying to remember exactly where he had seen her face.

Then it hit him... this was one of the chicks that Rocko had in the club house with him that night he was supposed to get with Pierre.

"I know you" Dontay said.

"Where you know me from?" She asked suspiciously.

"You came to my apartment with Rocko the other night."

"Oh, OK! Yeah, I remember you" They made small talk and then Javier asked... "Do you have any Iso?" He turned to Dontay and asked "What's it called again?

Dontay laughed then replied "Isotope."

"Iso... What???" Pam asked?

"Isotope." Dontay answered.

"Nah! I ain't got none of that shit. What's that anyhow?"

"Something I use to blow the coke up with" Dontay answered.

"I never even heard of that. What's the name of it again?"

"Alright Pam" Javier said before Dontay got a chance to repeat it cause whatever it is, he damn sure didn't want her to have it.

Dontay could tell that Javier didn't want to be in her presence any longer than he had to be but Dontay wanted to stay a few more minutes to try to pick her brain a little bit about Pierre.

"When Pierre coming back from Panama?" Dontay asked, just throwing the bait out there to see if she would bite.

"He's not in Panama. He still in town. As a matter of fact, he'll be over here later on tonight to pick up his daughter. You want me to tell him something?" Pam asked.

"Nah, I'll catch up with him later." Dontay replied.

"Alright then Pam." Javier said, still in a rush to get the fuck up out the hallway.

As they made their way back to the Blue Moon store, Dontay and Javier had a brief conversation about the cooking business.

"Look, I need to get some Isotope before I can do anything. I know where I can get some for chea, but you gotta let me know how much you try'na whip so I'll know how much to get."Dontay said.

"Me got 8 bricks. I'm trying to stretch dem as much as me can" Javier said.

"They're $250 a bottle and you're gonna need two bottles a brick. You said you got 8 joints so you're gonna need 16 bottles at $250 a bottle. That's 4 grand." Dontay said.

"No problem brethren. Let me holla at Rude Boy and when we're ready we'll hit ya on ya pager."Javier replied.

Dontay gave Javier his beeper number and gave him the code #8 to use for the number of keys he wanted whipped up.

When Dontay returned, JR and Rude Boy were sitting in front of the store high as a mutha fucker passing a fat splif.

"Come on slim, we gotta take care of this business." Dontay said

"Alright Rude Boy. It's always a pleasure brethren."JR said as he got up and slapped Rude Boy some dap.

"OK Brethren, ya be safe out here ya hear." Rude Boy said.

"Alright Brethren." Dontay said as he gave Rude Boy dap and walked towards the Beamer (BMW).

"Yes, Yes, Star! Ya be safe" Javier replied.

Dontay and JR jumped in JR's Beamer and burned rubber back up to Montana Housing Projects.

"Aye Slim. We got his ass!" Dontay said to JR.

"Got who?" JR asked.

"That nigga Pierre, what the fuck you mean who?" Dontay replied.

"HUH?" JR said.

Dontay looked over at JR who was higher than a satellite... "Man, you really need to slow down."

JR remained silent as he puffed on his joint, looking in Dontay's direction and blew out the weed smoke.

"Nevermind."Dontay said. Within minutes, they pulled up at the auto body garage on

Montana Avenue, where C.C. and Terry were waiting. Dontay got out of the Beamer with JR, then got into the car with C.C. and motioned Terry to follow them.

"Did you put the work in a good place?" Dontay asked?

"Yeah, It's safe." C.C. replied.

"Aiight good, let's go."

Dontay and C.C. pulled off with Terry following them. He informed C.C. about everything that he found out from the Jakes and the chick Pam. They laid out a plan of execution to stalk Pierre's girl's apartment until he showed up.

"I don't know about you big boi, but I plan on dumping every last single one of these hot ones into this rat bastard!"

They reached their destination and sat and waited for the rat to come out of his hole. The sun began to set, and the night air became chilly. They rode up and down the street, surveying the area to exterminate their little rodent problem.

"There she go right there slim! That's the chick Pam walking down the street holding the little girl's hand that answered the door earlier. Park right here." Dontay said.

They sat across the street from Pam's apartment building trying to remain as inconspicuous as possible behind the tinted windows, and waited for the rat Pierre to show his face.

Dontay felt his pager vibrating and glanced down at it. "This is Rocko. I ain't got time for him and his bullshit right now!" Dontay said.

They sat and waited for another two hours but Pierre was a no show.

"That nigga ain't coming. Let's roll out!" Dontay said. C.C. started the ignition and motioned for Terry to follow.

They were headed back down Georgia Ave, when Dontay spotted Pierre's white Porsche coming towards them.

"There that nigga go right there! Turn around!"

C.C. made a U-turn in the middle of Georgia Ave..."We got him slim!" Dontay said, then motioned for Terry to pull along-side of C.C.'s Fleetwood. Look here slim, there go the nigga right there. I want you to pull up in front of him and block him in so he can't pull off when I pull up on him.

Terry didn't say a word. He just followed Dontay's instruction, made his way through the traffic and pulled in front of Pierre's 944 Porsche.

C.C. eased the Fleetwood on the side of Pierre's Porsche to get Dontay as close as possible. Terry was in front and another car behind Pierre's Porsche. It made it impossible for him to get away.

C.C. pulled the Fleetwood right along-side of Pierre's Porsche; so close that Dontay could've reached out of the window and touched him.

The sound of the fully automatic gun fire made everyone standing around on the nearby sidewalk hit the deck and scramble in a frenzy for cover.

Pierre didn't stand a chance. 36 bullets from the Mack 11 ripped Pierre's face into shreds. C.C. looked over at Dontay and nodded his head in approval. He looked back through the rearview mirror to make sure that nobody was trying to follow him to get his tag number. Terry thought real quick to wave them past, then pulled the Fleetwood behind them as close as he could; making it hard for anyone to get the tag number.

****Breaking News****

Major Drug Dealer was gunned down tonight as a gunman in an unidentified vehicle pulled along-side of this white Porsche 944 and opened fire with a barrage of bullets. Witnesses that heard the gun shots say it sounded like a machine gun. However, police say that they don't have any eyewitnesses to the shooting, and urges anyone with information about the shooting to come forward.

Meanwhile, back at the station...

Captain Mark Torres stood there in the middle of the station dressed in his ordinary desert boots, Banana Republic khaki pants, safari vest over top of his desert storm camouflage t-shirt and safari bucket hat on his way fishing, when he received the news about

Pierre... "You mean to tell me that I have a dead informant out there in the streets with over 30 bullet holes in him, and no one seen shit? I'm really starting to question both of your skill levels out there in the field. Get back out there, eat in them streets, sleep in them streets and snatch up any and every low life piece of shit that jaywalks and bring them in for questioning until someone tells you anything we can use to bring these bastards in, and If neither one of you can make an arrest on this case and have Beltre' in my holding cell within 48 hours, I'm handing the case over to the Feds. Now get out of my office and get on you fucking job!" Captain Torres angrily spit at his 2 detectives Redman and Black. They turned on their heels and exited the office without saying a word because they knew they had dropped the ball bad on this one. The one real chance they had of making a solid arrest on Dontay and Rocko had evaporated in thin air like a cloud of smoke. They were back to square one and the frustration was mounting up at an all-time high. The ridicule, the jokes and the wisecracks from their fellow officers sitting around at their desks were making matters worse. Redman was fed up and he was ready to put his own over-zealous tactics into gear.

"Damn it!" Redman shouted out in boiling frustration "How did we let this happen?"

"It's not our fault Red. The C.I. played us from the jump.

"You think Dontay and Rocko found out somehow about Carter's cooperation and pumped 32 bullets in him?"

"Rocko naw, but Beltre is worth looking into because as it stands right now, we have nothing and the Cap is gonna have our asses hanging off the end of his fishing rod; feeding us to the fishes if we don't come up with something fast."

"Yeah, tell me about it." Detective Redman responded as they exited the station.

CHAPTER

EIGHTEEN

THE BEST OF BOTH WORLDS

"The right man is the one who seizes the moment at the right time." –SB

A few days later, Dontay pulled up on 15th Street, where C.C. was standing up against the fence getting his car washed.

"What's up big boi? Dontay asked as he slapped C.C. some dap."How it's looking up here?"

"Slow. You know your man Troy pulled up lookin' for you."

"Oh yeah, he came through here?"

"Yeah, he rode through about 10 minutes ago. He said call him ASAP. Here." He handed Dontay a Motorola cell phone. Dontay dialed the number and the phone just rung. "It gotta be important if he came through here. That nigga don't ever come to the hood. Shit! No answer."

He handed C.C. the phone. Minutes later Troy's black 928 Porsche with chrome classic rims came over the hill.

"There he go right there." C.C. said directing Dontay's attention to his left. Troy never came to the projects unless it was extremely necessary, so him showing unexpected had to be real serious. He still owed Troy money, but he was always good to come correct. Therefore, he wasn't sure what this unexpected visit was all about. Dontay took a deep breath, then stepped off the curb as Troy pulled up.

"What's up slim? What brings you out?" He asked when he leaned inside the passenger's side window not sure if he was ready for the answer.

"Get in!" He ordered and without hesitation, Dontay got into the passenger seat of the Porsche.

"You finished that work yet?"

"Nah, I ran into a minor delay but they'll be outta my hands in a day or two." Troy didn't trip about the delay because he knew Dontay had a strong enough team with the clientele to have the money when he said he would have it. Dontay solidified his position with Troy and earned his trust when he moved 50 keys for him in two months' time, and wasn't a dollar short. Dontay had jumped over Blue in status and positioned himself to push Julio completely out the picture. The 20 keys in 2 weeks that Blue promised he could deliver Julio was now a promise he could no longer keep without Dontay. The gold mine that Blue so badly wanted a piece of was now out of his reach, and caused him to seek out another alternative to manipulate his way into the projects.

"I got a promotion for you under one condition." Troy said.

"Oh yeah, what's condition is that?"

"You gotta have some restraint with that pistol out here and if you can do that, I'll throw you an alley-oop that'll put you in a position to sit down with Kelvin, and put you in play with my clientele. They'll have to come through you for what they want. You can even get that money from Julio if you want. But, in order for you to solidify that position, you would have to assume the risk of all logistics."

"What going on? What did I do to deserve this?"

"It's like this. You know when a light bulb has ran It's course for so long, that light starts to flicker out. That means it's time to replace that bulb. I'm moving on to bigger and better things these days. The objective is to get in, get enough paper to do something legit with it, and get out before the feds get it. You think you can shoulder the load?"

Dontay turned his attention away from Troy and stared out the windshield for a moment contemplating what was just dropped in his lap. This was the big break he was waiting for. Getting put on with a plug of this magnitude to a nigga in the streets, was like getting signed to a major league sports team. Troy continued to lay out the play just like a good coach would, preparing his star player for the playoffs and his championship run.

"This is all the info you need for now. He handed Dontay a piece of paper. "You'll check in the Mirage under that pseudonym on the paper and someone will get in touch with you. Remember to keep the Money, and the Murder separated because when you mix the two together, it brings too much Mayhem... you dig? If someone needs to be dealt with, hire a hitter that has no direct ties to you. Someone that the feds can't link back to you, understand? Julio just might be a good candidate for that position because nobody in these city streets knows him or his crew."

"I understand where you're coming from but I like to paint the house myself. Dontay exited the Porsche when it came to a stop on 15th street and walked towards C.C. who was waiting against the fence.

"Pack your bags big boi. We headed to Sin City!" He told C.C. and patted him on his shoulders, then got into his Mercedes and pulled off contemplating his new position and everything Troy said about leaving the violence for someone else to handle. This was the break he'd been dreaming of his entire life. He anticipated Julio and Blue feeling some kind of way about his come up and having to get their work from him, especially Julio, but what the fuck. It was his time to shine."Fuck their feelings!" He said to himself with a light laugh as he drove through the city listening to Earth Wind & Fire "Fantasy."

MONEY, MURDER & MAYHEM

Money, Murder & Mayhem consumed every aspect of his life, and it was no room in the world he lived in for a committed relationship. He liked Stacy and wanted to see exactly where she would fit into his life, but the streets had a hold on him right now that was too strong for him to break away.

He was on a serious paper chase, and had goals of seeing a million dollars cash by the time he was 21. Only then, would he would be done with the business for good. He often times contemplated the idea of one day having a family and a son, an heir to his throne. A prince he could teach how to play basketball, ride a bike, tie his shoes, and brush his teeth. The simple things in life that would mold his character and develop his manhood the way it was taught to him. He wondered what his life would be like without the hustle, but as the saying goes... "You keep your mind on your paper, bitches out your business, and your ears to the street."

CHAPTER

NINETEEN

THE POWERS THAT BE

"Power tends to corrupt, and absolute power corrupts absolutely, and there is no worse hearsay than that of the office that sanctifies the holder of it." –Lord Acton

---

"We been riding around for 3 freakin' days, and we ain't run across one person from off that hill that's willing to come in and tell us something on Dontay and the Montana boys."

"Yeah, I know. It's pathetic how scared these mutha fuckaz are of these sons of bitches."

Detective Black added to Redman's frustration.

"We can't catch a break. We just gotta take matters into our own hands."

"What do you mean by that?" Detective Black asked.

"What I mean is that if we can't do it their way, we'll do it our way. I'm tired of playing games with these sons of bitches out here. I'll put up half of my pension to see these sons of bitches in jail for the rest of their worthless lives or 6 feet under. Either way will give me the greatest satisfaction of my life."

"Wow! Listen to you... half of your pension huh? That's a heavy statement right there detective. Why is getting

Dontay and the Montana boys off the streets that important to you?" Detective Black turned to her partner and asked.

"Because! These sons of bitches piss more money than I make in a year. They're riding around in Mercedes, and wearing Rolex watches on their wrists that cost more than my got damn house. I work hard to make an honest living out here. I pay my taxes on time every year, and these sons of bitches sell dope, kill people and been getting away with it for far too long as far as I'm concerned. I'm tired of it. I'm gonna dedicate all my time, day and night until I get these sons of bitches." He retorted as he threw back a couple of anti-depression and anxiety pills. He was in search of something that the pills could not provide. Meaning, purpose, and relief from losing all hope and confidence in his ability to do his job. He came close to losing his cool many times before but, not being able to put the cuffs on Dontay and Rocko angered him to his breaking point, and he had to release the tension the greatest way he knew how. The only remedy for his anxiety was to get rid of Dontay and Rocko. To him, that was the best prescription.

Detective Black stares out of the window while her partner vented his preemptive intent and obvious frustrations, ruminating his malevolence and unethical intentions. She introspectively hung on to his every word, not agreeing with his intended approach. She wanted Dontay and the Montana boys off the streets just as bad as he did but, she wasn't willing to risk her career, without any regard for the meaning of "FIDELITY" on the shield that they represented. She took her complaint to the Captain when they arrived back at the station.

"Cap, I think Redman is becoming a little too obsessed with Dontay and the Montana boys.

Yesterday, after we sat and waited for over 5 hours at the Cloisters Apartment Complex, he became frustrated and vexed about not being able to get them off the streets, and started talking about doing things his way. I want them off the streets too but, I wanna be able to live with myself and be able to sleep at night knowing that I did my job the right way. Cap, he's losing it and I'm just scared that he's gonna do something stupid that he will later regret."

"Alright detective. Thanks for bringing your concerns forward. I'll talk to him. We can't have that. This department doesn't do things that way. We have one of the highest arrest and conviction rates in the city and I'll be damned if I'm gonna have one frustrated Detective ruin that reputation. Tell Redman I wanna see him in my office right now!"

Detective Black walked out to inform her partner of her infidelity and tried to convince him that it's for his own good, and that she only reported him to the Captain because she loved him, and didn't want him to do something stupid. The Capitan gave Detective Redman a leave of absence till further notice, to give him time to clear his head and calm down.

"Look you're a good Detective, one of the best that I have in this department, but, I don't think you're using clear judgment in dealing with this case. So, I'm gonna need you to turn in your badge and service weapon, and I'm putting you on a leave of absence with pay: Effective Immediately." Detective Redman didn't say a word as he removed his badge from his waist and took his gun out of his shoulder holster. His mind was made up as far he was concerned; Dontay and Rocko were good as dead. He sat his badge and gun on the Captain's desk, then turned and walked out of the Captain's office as he walked past the other detectives quietly sitting at their desk, not surprised in the least at the Capitan's decision to fire Redman.

He looked his now ex-partner right in the eye, disgusted by her treachery. Without saying a word, he walked over to his desk and grabbed the gym bag from the drawer, then proceeded over to his ignominious ex-partner at the coffee machine. He slapped the shit out of her as hard as he could. He then walked out of the station, got into his car, popped a couple of pills; then furiously sped off. Leaving smoke, and skid marks in the parking lot.

He banged furiously on his steering wheel at the stop light out of sheer anger before speeding off into traffic. Running the red light causing cars to beep their horns, slamming on brakes, and swerving to keep from hitting him.

CHAPTER TWENTY

THE FED IS WATCHING

"Conscience is the inner voice which warns us that someone may be lurking in the shadows." -H.L. Mencken

After calming himself down a little, Detective Redman pulled up to an old house on V street N.W., parked his car and lit his cigarette. He pulled out his personal snub nose .38 from his ankle holster, checked to see if it was loaded then stuck it into his shoulder holster. Sat there and stared at the house for a second before getting out of the car and making his way to the front door. He peeped through the window to see if anyone was inside and spotted an older woman walking towards the kitchen. He pushed the door bell and watched through the window as the woman made her way towards the door. He fumbled with the pistol in his shoulder holster to make sure it didn't fall out. The woman looked out the window with curiosity in her eyes as to who the pale faced, square chinned blond hair, white man was at her door.

"May I help you?" She asked.

"Yeah, how are you Ma'am? I'm here to see Purcell White."

"I don't know anyone by that name." "I assure you, I'm not here to cause any trouble Ma'am. I'm a friend of his and need to talk to him about some business. Tell him Detective Redman is here to see him." Without saying a word she closed the curtain and walked away. A few minutes later the door opens.

"Well, well, well, look what the old cat dragged in." Scar said as he stepped aside to let Detective Redman into his humble abode.

"What brings you on this side of town?"

"Is it somewhere we can talk in private?" Scar stared at him for a second and knew that this private conversation was more than a social visit from his old partner. It was no doubt in his mind that this visit was about some serious business. Business that Scar was in no shape to consider at this point and time in his life.

"You want a drink Detective?"

"Yeah, make it a double of your strongest."

"Sounds like you had a rough day, what's going on?" Scar asked not really sure if he was ready to hear the answer because what he remembers about Detective Redman, was that they don't come any more corrupt than him, and the last time he did a job for him, he nearly lost his life and wears a colostomy bag till this day.

"I got a job for you. It's real easy work that shouldn't take you no more than a day or two."

"You know I'm retired from that life Detective" Scar said as he handed Redman his double shot of Jack Daniels.

Yeah I know, but I know you and you're not the type to sit around feeling sorry for yourself and become decrepit. Besides, I know you can use the money."

"How much we talkin' bout detective?"

Redman took a sip of his drink, then frowned his face as the alcohol burned the inside of his chest as it made its way down his throat.

"Damn, that's some strong shit." He sat his glass down, sat back in his chair, crossed his legs and pulled an envelope full of cash out of his blazer and placed it on the table.

"I got two targets. $50 grand a piece and 3 kilos. Half now, and the rest when the job is complete. You interested?"

"You haven't come this hard since you wanted the mother fuckers that stole your "**Blue Bags**." Who are they?" Scar asked as he took a sip of his Jack Daniels.

"A couple of local hustlers up on Montana Terrace." He said, then slid a manila folder across the table towards Scar. Scar opened the folder and stared at the photos for a second.

"Montana again huh? These guys look young." Scar said as he looked down at the photos.

"Yeah but don't let those young faces fool you. These kids are wealthy, and as dangerous as they come, and they're in my way."

Detective Redman reached inside his blazer and pulled out a small piece of paper and pushed it across the table.

"This is their last fixed address. Make it quick, but painful he said as he stood up."

Stacy heard voices in the kitchen when she made her way up the stairs from the basement carrying a laundry basket full of clothes. She walked in on the end of their conversation but quickly noticed the sudden movement from her dad, when he made an attempt to hide the pictures that were on the table. However, she was able to get a glimpse of the photos of Dontay.

"Oh. I'm sorry for interrupting, she said. I didn't know we had company. I just need to get the laundry powder out of the pantry and I'll be outta your way."

"Well that's my time. Good to see you again partner." Detective Redman said as he extended his hand towards Scar. The two men shook hands briefly.

"If you wanna take that fishing trip with me for old time sake, give me a holla. It'll be fun. Don't let life pass you by partner."Redman said with a smirk on face in an attempt to throw Stacy off just in case she was curious as to why he was there.

"I'll be in touch detective. Thanks for stopping by." Scar then showed Redman out and closed the door behind him then turned around to see Stacy staring at him.

"What that detective want? I know he not trying to get you to come back on the force after what happened to you."

"No. That's not it. That's not it at all. He just needed my help on a case he trying to solve, that's all. Don't worry. I hung up my gun and badge a long time ago. I'll never leave your side again."

He said in a reassuring tone to keep her out of his real business.

Stacy looked down at the envelope in his hand and the curiosity as to why the detective would give her dad a picture of Dontay was eating at her like Cancer. She knew she would never get a straight answer from him so she needed to talk to the one person that could at least scratch her curiosity itch. She paged Dontay 911 and impatiently waited for him to call. All kinds of thoughts crossed her mind while she folded clothes, and periodically glanced over at the phone. Her curiosity quickly turned into concern when Dontay didn't call right back. She worried that he was in some kind of trouble and prayed that he wasn't a dangerous drug dealer. She had developed a hatred for drug dealers after her dad told her that he had to wear a colostomy bag on his stomach for the rest of his life, as the result of being shot in the line of duty by a drug dealer. She was snapped out of her train of thought when the phone ranged. She dropped her clothes and anxiously answered the phone.

"Hello!"

"Hey! Good lookin'! What's up with you?"

"I'm fine, how are you?" She asked with a smile on her face. She was always happy to hear his voice and relieved to know that he was safe. She wanted to ask him the one question, but she worried about that answer because she really liked him. He cut her off before she could even fix her lips to spit it out.

"Get dressed. I got a little surprise for you. I'll be there in 20 minutes." Then he hung up.

Shortly after their brief conversation, Dontay pulled up at Renee's house and beeped the horn.

Scar opened the front door and looked through the screen at the car but was cut off by

Stacy before he could make any attempt to step out of the doorway.

"That's my ride, excuse me." She rushed passed Scar, giving him a playful nudge as she made her way out the door.

"Who the hell you got coming to pick your fast ass up now?"

"Didn't they teach you how to mind your business at that fancy school you went to?" She replied with a mild laugh in her tone and a hint of antagonism to throw his own words back in his face after she received the same unpleasant response from him.

Dontay sat and watched Stacy as she walked with grace towards to car, hips swaying from side to side as if she was a runway model on the cat walk. She wasn't the type he usually went after, but she had the body that'll give any stripper a run for her money. Everything was well proportioned on her 5'5" frame but often times kept it covered up with baggy jeans and big shirts. She was smart and had a natural knack for business. Her style was basic but with his taste and money, he would make her one of the flyest chicks DC had ever seen.

"You look nice." He said as she got in the car.

"Thank you, you look nice too. What's this surprise you got for me?"

"You'll see." He said then pulled off.

They both had a thing for seafood, so he suggested they stop to grab something from a small, cozy little seafood joint on Georgia Ave. They sat at the bar and ordered a couple of shrimp salads and played around with a plate of oysters that neither of them could swallow. Anxious to know what Dontay had in store for her, she pressed on. He looked at his watch and smiled.

You ready to go? He asked.

"Am I gonna get my surprise now?" He laughed, then stood up and paid the bill for their food. Come on let's get outta here.

They left the restaurant hand in hand. She started to feel comfortable, safe and secure in his presence and laughed at herself when she remembered how paranoid she was to think that he was dangerous. He was sweet and kind to her. She was comfortable with him. He treated her nice and made her feel sexy. Exactly the type of boyfriend she had been looking for.

The thought of telling him what she saw the detective give her father crossed her mind, but she was having such a good time, she didn't want to ruin their day. They got into his Mercedes and drove on Interstate 270 through Tyson's Corner to Dulles airport. Stacy looked puzzled, and unsure of what exactly Dontay had planned; but she felt confident and secure that she was in good hands and put her paranoia to rest.

Dontay drove through the security check and around the airport hanger, and was greeted by the airport security guard. He showed the security guard his clearance. Looked over at Stacy and smiled. She looked confused.

"Right this way Sir." The security guard said, then led the way towards the private Gulfstream G65OER Learjet; where the Pilot and the flight attendant waited his arrival for his complementary flight to Vegas, thanks to Troy and Courtesy of the Mirage Casino and Hotel. He grabbed his and Stacy's carry-on bag from the trunk and boarded the jet. Where C.C. and his girl Rhonda had already made themselves comfortable.

"Oh My God! This is so beautiful!" She said as she looked around. The flight attendant came on board and offered them a glass of champagne before going into the cockpit.

"I knew you would like this but this isn't the surprise. There's more to come." Stacy took a sip of her Champagne and looked out the window as the jet made its way to the runway for take-off.

"Where we going?" She curiously asked?

"You trust me right?" Dontay replied while operating without a fraction of trust for her or anyone outside of his crew for that matter.

"Yeah, I trust you!" She answered.

"Then just relax and enjoy the flight."

Stacy was not the type of person to assume, but her suspicions started to set in a little deeper and she wondered how he was able to afford such an expensive lifestyle. She hoped he wasn't a drug dealer. She was never impressed with material things and just couldn't see how they thought it was cool to profit from the destruction of their own community. She believed that drug dealers who considered themselves smart were actually oxymoron's to believe that they would be successful in life from selling illegal narcotics; when most of them share the same fate of either in the ground or in a jail cell. DC's homicide's rate was well over 400 and she didn't want to attach herself to someone who took those kinds of risks with his life. She just didn't want to be a part of that world.

She loved dick too much to have it locked away from her for 20 years, so she had to ask before she allowed herself to fall in love with someone that could be snatched away from her at any time. "How can you afford all this?" She wondered and braced herself for the answer.

"I was fortunate enough to reap the benefits of my dad's will/life insurance. He owned a construction company and passed away when I was eleven and my mother took over the company for a while but, eventually sold it to pursue her passion in real estate." He lied to keep her completely oblivious to his lifestyle. She was relieved that his life didn't involve anything illegal so she thought...and at that very moment, her paranoia and suspicion were removed from her mind.

While the jet was in mid-air she looked back at C.C. and Rhonda, who were engaging in their very own mile high, sexual exploits. "Never mind them." Dontay told her, and right on cue, she made her way over to him and sat on his lap. She wrapped her arms around his neck and gently kissed him on the lips.

"No one ever treated me like this before."

"Well, you might as well get used to it." They began kissing passionately and she wanted him in the worse way. She couldn't believe how quick she was so willing to give it up. Her pussy got wet and began to throb for him. She didn't worry about being caught by the flight attendant because in her mind this was an experience of a lifetime that she was not going to miss out on.

She reached down to grab his dick and he was already at full erection. She wasn't a dick canister, but he was packing the biggest dick she had ever seen in her young life. She unzipped his pants and was staring at 8 1/2 inches of grade "A" all American beef.

She got on her knees in between his legs and wrapped her pretty lips around his manhood. She slowly moved her mouth up and down on him, then twirled her tongue around the tip. Dontay sat there with his eyes closed enjoying the feeling of getting his dick sucked 30 thousand miles in the air. The warmth of her mouth and her superb oral technique caused him to moan as he came close to climax. Stacy continued to suck and lick all around his dick with voracity, savoring every inch of him until she felt his legs shaking...bringing him to that moment of satisfaction. He couldn't believe the skills Stacy possessed with her tongue, nor how quick she got on her knees in front of C.C. and Rhonda.

Stacy enjoyed giving head. She had practiced long nights with her pink dildo to become what she considered herself as The Master of The Ultimate Oral Experience, and waited for the chance to unleash the beast on who she deemed worthy.

CHAPTER

TWENTYONE

THE CITY THAT NEVER SLEEPS

"Nothing was ever accomplished while you slept." –Don Juan

The jet landed at exactly 4:00pm on a scorching hot Friday afternoon at Las Vegas McCarran International Airport, and the humidity was no joke. Their first thoughts were to get out of their clothes and get into something more comfortable and take refuge under the air conditioner. They got their rental cars and drove to the Mirage Casino and Hotel located on the main strip where they had reservations for Presidential suites. C.C. got the suit cases from the trunk and he and Rhonda headed straight to their room. The girls were in Vegas for pleasure but this was a business trip for Dontay and at every turn, C.C. made sure he reminded him.

When they stepped inside the hotel, the ambiance was a thing of beauty. The craftsmanship was a work of art and the staff was surprisingly friendly to a couple of young blacks from the projects. After checking in, Dontay and Stacy went to the crap table. Dontay didn't gamble, but this was Stacy's very first time in Vegas and he wanted her to enjoy herself and have the best time of her life. He gave her $3,000 to start with. She got the dice and placed her bet. Her first roll landed on 6. "The point for the young lady is 6." The table conductor yelled. Raked the dice back in with the table stick and pushed them back over to Stacy. She rolled a couple more times then hit her point.

"We have a winner!" The table conductor yelled. Stacy got excited and kissed Dontay on the cheek.

"Oh my God! I won!" She said with excitement, then rolled the dice again. The point was 4 and she bucked that number after a few more rolls of the dice. Stacy began to jump up and down from her overwhelming experience of being in Vegas and winning money. Shortly after collecting their winnings from the crap table, they headed to their suite on the 18th floor. The suite was lavish and spacious with a king size bed and Jacuzzi with a view overlooking the outdoor swimming pool, and the boxing ring at the neighboring hotel Caesar's Palace. The moment they set foot back in their room, Dontay hugged her from behind then blindfolded her with the napkins around the ice bucket and led her to the bed. He grabbed a bowl of strawberries from the sex essential gift basket, and a bottle of mango flavored body oil; complements of the hotel.

Then slowly undressed her, and began to rub small amounts of oil all over her body. The touch of his hands on her soft delicate skin was gentle and sensual. She let out a harmonious moan when he touched her vagina. He paused momentarily and grabbed a strawberry from the bowl and took a small bite before rubbing the other half across her lips. He put the strawberry in his mouth and fed it to her with a kiss so he could taste the sweet nectar of the fruit on her soft lips. He wanted to give her the ultimate experience and enjoy her in every way possible. So he reached for the bottle of chocolate syrup, and put small drops on the nipples of her 34D size breast, then sucked them clean. He kissed and licked chocolate off every curve of her body, and dug a little deeper into his bag of tricks. He reached over on the night- stand and grabbed an ice cube from the ice bucket that kept the bottle of champagne on chill, and rubbed it gently across her breast. The cold sensation sent a chill up her spine. He put the ice cube into his mouth and glided it from the top of her shoulder, down her breast to her stomach; then taking his talents to South Beach. He glided the ice across the lips of her pussy, then licked her clit until the tingling sensation caused her body to tremble. He began to simultaneously lick her pussy and her ass until she screamed for the Lord... "Oh my God!"

"No baby, not God...Dontay!"He said with a mix of confidence and arrogance.

He began to suck on her clit and twirl his tongue more forcefully. She snatched the blindfold off her eyes and tried to escape his grasp, but he wasn't done with her yet. He wanted to conquer her, and get her so sprung that she'll eventually accept his way of life when he told her about his drug dealing, murderous lifestyle. No one had ever licked her pussy and ass at the same time before and made her cum as hard as she did. He could tell from the way she looked at him, that he had done more than satisfied her. After his award winning pussy and ass eating performance, they fucked well into the wee hours of the night from the bed, to the shower, to the balcony, to the floor, and ended on the kitchen table. This was one night she would surely never forget.

The next morning they met up with C.C. and Rhonda in the lobby and went on a shopping spree at the Venetian. They hit every major boutique you could think of that was happening, from Gucci, Fendi, Versace, Armani, M.C.M & Hugo Boss. You name it. If it was high fashion, they had to have it.

They had more bags than their hands could carry. This was only their second day in Sin City and they we're burning the strip up. They went to grab a bite at the Ming Terrace, inside the Imperial Palace and dined on the best seafood platter on the planet, where Stacy surprised him with a solid gold rope necklace with a diamond encrusted medallion, which bore initials.

Dontay's beeper started vibrating like crazy. It was Troy's code with an unfamiliar number. Dontay got up from the table and grabbed the first pay phone he saw, and dialed the digits. A raspy voice picked up the phone on the other end and told him to meet him at the Flamingo Hotel, room 809 in an hour and to come alone (click)! He looked down at his Rolex watch, then walked back to the table where C.C. and the girls waited patiently for his return. Not wanting to give the girls any indication of what they were really in Vegas for, he gave C.C. a head nod, tapped his watch and held up his index finger. He pulled out his bank roll and peeled off enough money for the bill. "Let's get these bags back to the room." Dontay said then stood up with as many bags his two hands could carry. Stacy and Rhonda were getting acquainted and talking up a storm when C.C. asked Dontay about the call. He wanted me to come alone to the Flamingo Hotel, room 809, in one hour. I'll be in the lobby waiting for you and keeping my eyes open for them peoples, C.C. said. Get the girls back to the hotel and give them some money so they can keep themselves busy.

I'll meet you outside in front of the Volcano in 45 minutes.

Once they arrived back to the Mirage Hotel and Casino, Dontay grabbed the bags from Stacy and told her he had to go take a shit, and that he would take the bags up to the room and for her to go with C.C.

Stacy was having a pretty good conversation with Rhonda and getting to know her was pretty easy because they had a lot in common, so she didn't put up any objection to his order and simply obliged without an inkling of a clue as to what he might be up to or involved in.

As soon as he got to his room, he dumped all the clothes out of the shopping bags onto the bed, replaced them with the 250 thousand, then put the clothes on top. Within minutes, he was back down stairs and had the valet bring his rental car. Ten minutes later, he pulled in front of the Flamingo Hotel.

He casually walked through the lobby and got on the elevator. He pushed the button for the 8th floor, but before the elevator door closed. A white hand reached out between the doors causing the doors to open. In steps two white men dressed in shorts, tank tops and sunglasses. Dontay suspected them to be the cops at first glance but, quickly erased that notion once he didn't see a badge or gun holster, and they were both wearing thong flip flops. The white men got off the elevator on the 8th floor. They were ahead of Dontay and headed left down the long hallway. Dontay stepped out of the elevator with caution and watched the two men until they were out of his view. Then he proceeded down the right side of the hallway. Stepped in front of room 809 and put his ear to the door to hear the voices inside. The sound of the "Price is Right" television game show was all he heard. His knock went unanswered so, he put his ear to the door again then raised his fist to knock again when the door opened and there stood Kelvin in a white Gucci bath robe.

"Right on time." Kelvin said as he turned and walked towards the table where he sat down facing Dontay.

"I see you did a little shopping on your way here huh?"

"Yeah, something like that." Dontay replied. Their meeting was relaxed and comfortable because Troy had stamped Dontay in a major way, but since this was the first time Kelvin had dealt with Dontay directly, he was reluctant to push too much off on him at once. He wanted to see if Dontay was all that Troy said he was. Dontay negotiated a price at 15.5 per key under the condition that he would have all his money in 30 days. Kelvin agreed to the terms, and Dontay handed him the shopping bag.

"What's this?" Kelvin asked.

"It's the $250,000 and the Versace shirt is for you. I'll have the rest in a few weeks."

Kelvin looked inside the bag, and then looked back up at Dontay with a smile.

"I dig your style. If you're about your business like Troy said you are, this just might work out."

"Wait right here." Kelvin turned and went into the bathroom and came back carrying a large suitcase. He sat it on the table and opened it. His demeanor was solid. The look in his eyes was serious, and the tone of his voice was firm. "ONE MONTH!" He said.

Dontay took the keys out of the suitcase and placed them into the shopping bag. He left Kelvin's room with 50 keys and a $500 thousand dollar bill hanging over his head. If he never felt pressure before, he felt it now. There was no room for any fuck-ups! C.C. was standing in the lobby looking at post cards in the gift shop when he saw Dontay getting off the elevator with two shopping bags. With all the gambling going on in the hotel and everyone preoccupied minding their own business, they made it out of the hotel unsuspected of anything out of the ordinary. The valet pulled their rental cars around and they headed back to the Mirage Hotel.

CHAPTER
TWENTYTWO

MONEY, POWER & RESPECT

"Money and Violence speaks sense in a language that all of mankind understands." —SB

After he concluded his business with Kelvin, they were on the jet headed back to D.C. Stacy boarded the jet at Dulles airport a mediocre, bamma dressing chick, and stepped off the jet one of the flyest bitches D.C. would ever see. She was wearing a pair of Versace jeans, black calf length, high heel Versace boots, 4 carat diamond earrings and a tennis bracelet to match. Diamond encrusted, baby face oyster perpetual Rolex, Chanel handbag, and a full length black and smoke gray Gucci trench coat that was suitable for the pouring rain back in D.C.

Shortly after their plane landed, they loaded their luggage in the trunk of his car. Stacy was getting into the passenger seat when she noticed through the rear window Dontay and C.C. putting guns in the waistbands of their pants. She sat in the passenger seat and remained quiet about what she saw but was becoming more suspicious about

Dontay's lifestyle and why he needed a gun. Curiosity began to eat away at the interrogator. She laid the car seat back, laid her head on the head rest and closed her eyes. With C.C. in tow, Dontay drove to his mother's house. Once the car came to a stop and Stacy heard Dontay get out of the car, she peeped through her half closed eyes at the side view mirror and saw Dontay taking the suitcase out of the trunk and overheard his conversation with C.C.

"It's no time to be bullshitting out here. We need to get this work in the hands of the folks that's about their business, so we can get that money back to Vegas ASAP!"

The sound of the trunk slamming put her back in "pretending to be sleep" mode.

Dontay looked over at Stacy and noticed she was asleep as they took the suitcases in the house. Totally unaware that she was faking, she peeped his movements and watched him and C.C. go inside the house; she suspected Dontay was involved in more than he led her to believe. She continued to "fake sleep" when Dontay got back in the car, and after driving for another 10 minutes, they arrived at Stacy's house.

"Wake up sleepy head!" He said as he put his hand on her thick thigh. Stacy opened her eyes.

"We here already?"

"Yeah! You were knocked out!"

"I had a wonderful time with you this weekend and thank you so much for all the gifts you bought me."

"Don't mention it! I'm just glad I was able to put a smile on your pretty face and show you a good time." Then he leaned over, removed her hair from her face and kissed her passionately.

Scar's car pulled up on the opposite side of the street. He sat there for a moment and looked over at the Mercedes he saw his daughter get into a couple days ago. He grabbed his gun from the glove compartment and put it in the pocket of his hoody. He put the hood over his bald head, got out of the car and began walking in their direction with his hands inside his hoody pocket, firmly gripping his pistol.

"Shit! That's my nosey ass father!" Scar walked in front of the Mercedes but his view was obscured from the pouring rain. He motioned for her with a hand gesture to get out of the car. Then turned on his heels and began walking towards the house.

"Call me later." She said.

"I will, you want me to help you with your bags?"

"No! I got it, thanks." Dontay opened the trunk as she got out of the car so she could retrieve her bags. As soon as he heard the trunk slam shut – **play time was over!** Dontay pulled off and it was time to get to work!

While Dontay was headed to meet up with C.C. to put the word out that they were back in business. Stacy was getting the third degree from her father "What's all this? He asked when he looked at her and noticed the expensive clothes she had on, and all the clothes she had in the bags on the floor.

"What did I tell your lil fast ass about messing with them drug dealers?"

"I told you before, he's not a drug dealer." Stacy replied.

"How the hell can he afford to drive a Mercedes like that, and buy you all these fancy and expensive clothes if he ain't out there slinging that shit?"

"His father passed away when he was a kid. He and his mother inherited his construction company, that's how!"

"Ha, Ha, Ha! Is that what he told you?" He said shaking his head in disbelief at his daughter's naivety and lack of street knowledge.

"Girl, you're greener than the grass outside and this guy got your nose wide open."

"Why are you so negative? Everyone that drives a nice car or has money is not a drug dealer dad."

"You're right, but, what do you really know about this guy? He could be a serial killer."

"A serial killer dad? Really?"

"I'm just saying, you never know."

"He's not a serial killer dad! Once you meet him, you'll see for yourself."

"That's a good idea! Why don't you invite him over for dinner so I can meet this nice guy that got my daughter so sprung. That way, I can see for myself if he's worthy of you or if he's noxious to you."

"I'm not sprung dad, and I don't know what noxious means but, you really need to get a life."

She retorted then turned and walked away."

CHAPTER
TWENTYTHREE

FRIEND OR FOE

"Set honor in one eye and death in the other and I will look upon them both indifferently and ask God to speed up my demise in the name of HONOR if I ever betrayed a friend." –SB

Shortly after dropping Stacy off at her house, he got straight to business and met with his regular clientele. He hit them off with keys for 23 grand per unit. Within a few days, 20 of the 50 keys he received from Kelvin were gone, and he banked in $460,000. He was still $40,000 short of the $500,000 he owed Kelvin but, had $690,000 worth of product left out there on the streets.

He pulled the $40 grand out of his own stash to put with the $460,000 and booked a flight to Vegas to make the drop off. Word quickly spread throughout the streets that Dontay had bricks for cheap, and while he was distributing the coke throughout the city's up and coming young hustlers, Rocko felt slighted that he got overlooked so he put his own play in motion and reached out to Julio to make his own move, not knowing that Julio had a totally different agenda once he peeped a weakness in Rocko that night at the Metro Club, when he joined him in treating his nose to a one on one; when began spilling his guts about Dontay's business. Julio sat quietly and smoked his cigarette, listening to Rocko express his gripe about being loyal and still got looked over. Julio laid out another line of coke for Rocko to snort. "Don't sweat it my man. I got you. I just might be the solution to your problem my man. I'm looking to purchase 20 keys and if you could get me a meeting with your man Dontay, it might be beneficial for the both of us. I get what I want, you get what you want, and we both walk away happy men."

That's what I'm talking about! Sounds good to me." Rocko said then leaned forward to snort the line of coke. Julio sat back and watched him with malicious intentions as Rocko snorted line after line of the white powder while the Mick Jenkins song "Drowning" blasted from the speakers.

Minutes after his meeting with Julio, Rocko called Dontay to set up a meeting to discuss what he hoped would be the break he'd been waiting for. Rocko wanted out of Dontay's shadow and his own position in the game as a major player. Dontay agreed to meet with him at the Langston Park swimming pool at 11pm because after all, Rocko was still someone he considered family. When he arrived, Dontay was already there swimming laps as he always does with one of his men standing guard with the Mack- 11 semi-automatic. Dontay noticed Rocko standing at the edge of the pool talking to C.C. while he continued to swim laps.

Rocko was smart, and was once known in the hood as "The Coke Connoisseur" because of his unique talent to be able to eyeball anything from an ounce to a key, and never be more than a gram off. He taught Dontay a lot about the business, and he felt deserving of more than what Dontay was giving him. In a number of ways he was right, but Rocko was slipping bad and Dontay peeped it, this is why he gave Rocko a less involved role before his mistakes caused them their freedom or worse.

He came to Dontay with a deal on the table that he felt would set him up nice, and put him in a position to branch off and do his own thing.

Dontay got out of the pool where Rocko and C.C. were standing, and grabbed a towel.

"What's good?" He asked Rocko as he dried off.

"Listen, I got a real sweet lick with a couple of out of towners for 20 of them thangs at 25 a joint. I figured, you can use the help to get rid of some of them joints you sitting on."

"Use some help!?" Dontay laughed… "Naw playboy, I'm good. I got all the help I need. We all know how that last deal you put together ended and how do you know these niggaz from out of town is for real?"

"Well as it turns out, you happen to know these niggaz."

"Is that right, who are they?"

"Your New York man Blue, and the Puerto Rican."

"Blue and Juilo huh?"

Dontay's mind wandered as to why Blue would go through Rocko to cop, and not come straight to him. Something didn't seem right about this move, and he really didn't want to entertain the thought of allowing Rocko anywhere close to the inner-dealings of his business after that slip with Pierre. He was one of his early teachers that educated him with a lot of the knowledge he has about the business, so against his better judgment, he agreed to let Rocko orchestrate the deal. It worked for him because he hadn't seen Blue in a minute and it would give them a chance to reconnect.

"O.K. Set up the meeting and let me know when and where. I'll meet you there."

CHAPTER

TWENTYFOUR

LIVIN' LA VIDA LOCA

"Call no man a FOE without first knowing him." —SB

Rocko set up the meeting at an apartment that Julio and Blue had rented while they stay in the city. They arrived at the apartment shortly after midnight, and as always, Dontay proceeded with the highest degree of caution and strapped up with his chrome 40 millimeter with an extra 16 shot clip and his bullet proof vest. It didn't matter to him that he was meeting with someone he considered a brother because in the streets, it was more times than none that it would be the ones you least expect to stab you in the back.

Rocko knocked on the door and was greeted by Julio "Que pa so mi amigo." He said and shook Rocko's hand. His facial expression changed in a split second at the sight of Dontay. "What's good kid?" He asked... masking his true feelings of disdain.

He never liked Julio for the obvious reason that he knew Julio didn't like him, and he wouldn't hesitate to empty his clip in Julio's face. Julio sat down on the leather love seat up against the wall facing the door, when Blue came from the back room. He embraced Dontay, but the feeling wasn't the same. A sense of uneasiness settled on him and he wasn't in the mood for the small talk. He was there to conduct business and get outta there with what he came for. "Relax kid. We're all family here." Blue said. But the look on Julio's face revealed something different. "Let's get this business out the way then we can have our little family reunion."

Julio sucked on his teeth as Dontay stood firm in his position not to let his guard down.

"Okay, fair enough. A business man! I respect that!" Blue said rubbing his hands together...

"What kind of numbers we talkin' bout?"

"For you! I can do 10 for a buck 80."

"A buck 80?! Come on baby! I know you can do me better than that after all we been through."

"That's the lowest I can go. Take it or leave it!"

"Take it or leave it huh!? O.K. He said as he stared at Dontay, and rubbed his hand over his mouth "Is that the work right there?" He asked and nodded his head towards the backpack Dontay was holding.

"You'll find out once I know that paper is correct." Dontay spat back him.

Julio's temper was starting to over flow and waited for the right moment to shoot Dontay and take what he felt was suppose to be his.

".*Ve por el dinero, voy a dispararle en la cabeza y tomarlo de todos modos.*" (i.e.) "Go get the money, I'm going to shoot him in the head and take it anyway." Julio said. Unaware that

Dontay understood every word, and at that very moment his thoughts began to travel a hundred miles per hour; in a million different directions as the Temptations song "Smiling Faces" popped in his mind when he looked over at Blue. Without warning, he smacked Blue across the face with the barrel of his pistol knocking him up against the wall, then quickly turned the gun on Julio and pumped 7 bullets into his chest. Rocko jumped back in disbelief as to what just happened **"WHAT THE FUCK!?"** He said at this unexpected burst of gunshots that rung out right in front of his face.

Blue rushed Dontay and grabbed him in a desperate attempt to get the gun from him to possibly save his own life. They struggled momentarily until a single shot to the abdomen put an end to all movement. Blue struggle for air as he tried to hold on to Dontay's shirt, but slowly fell to ground at Dontay's feet as his soul began to leave his body.

"Why the fuck you do that?" Rocko asked as he looked at the bodies then back at Dontay.

"Nigga I saved your life. You should be thanking me?" He spat back totally unaware that

Rocko was down with the lick. "While you was standing over there all "Happy Go-Friendly" and shit, these niggaz was talkin' bout smoking us. Go search the room." Dontay ordered. Rocko stood there unresponsive to Dontay's demands until he pointed his weapon in his direction...

"Go search the fuckin' room!"

The sound of voices in the hallway from neighbors that heard the gun shots quickly changed their course of direction.

"Fuck it! Come on let's go!" Dontay said.

They covered their faces as they stepped into the hallway only to hear the sound of doors slamming shut as neighbors didn't want to be seen and be exterminated as a potential witness.

"No Face, No Case!"

Once inside the car, Dontay began to unstrap his bullet proof vest and noticed that his necklace was gone "Shit!" He said out loud, feeling around his neck.

"What's wrong?"

"Nothing! Keep driving."

The 911 call came through on the dispatcher and Detectives Black and her new partner responded to the call. Upon arrival, the young rookie officer approached and debriefed them about the crime scene as they walked into the building.

"We got one deceased male with 7 holes to his upper torso. At this time, it doesn't seem like a robbery cause there's no sign of forced entry and nothing appears to be out of place. We recovered another shell casing and inspected the entire apartment, but there is no sign of where that bullet could've went."

"Good job officer. We'll take it from here. Detective Black told the young rookie.

Other officers were dusting the apartment for finger prints while they scanned it for another 30 minutes, when a call came across their radio that a gunshot victim just walked into Med Star trauma unit at Washington Hospital Center. They didn't hesitate to jump right on top of the call.

"This could be who got that other bullet in him." Detective Black said as they got into their car and burned rubber to the hospital. When they arrived, the victim was taken to emergency surgery. They showed the badges to the receptionist at the desk and asked about the gunshot victim that was just admitted. She directed their attention to the doctor standing in the middle of the hallway reading from the clipboard in his hand.

"Excuse me Doc." Detective Black said as she and her partner approached him. "I'm Detective Black and this is my partner Detective Swan."

"I'm Doctor Emmerson. Nice to meet you detectives. I assume you're here about the gunshot victim." "As a matter of fact, we are." "Follow me." He said, then led the way down the hall "We did everything we could to save him but unfortunately the shot to the abdomen was at close range and caused severe damage to his intestines and liver. He lost an astronomical amount of blood. Had he made it here 10 minutes earlier, he might've had a chance." Doctor Emmerson said as he pulled back the curtain and there lay, DEA Special Investigating Officer, Victor Rodriguez a.k.a. "Blue!" "We ran his prints through central because he didn't have any identification on him and it came back that he was a Special Officer with the DEA from New York. We have all of his belongings, but one interesting thing was he came in with a necklace tightly clutched in his hand. Maybe it can be of some help with this case." The doctor handed Detective Black the property bag containing the popped gold necklace with the diamond encrusted medallion.
"Thanks Doc. You been a great help."

They left the hospital on their way back to the station and Detective Black couldn't stop looking at the necklace in the plastic bag. Once at her desk, she tacked it to her board and stared at it for over an hour... "Talk to me baby!" She said as she stared at the necklace.

CHAPTER

TWENTYFIVE

IT'S SO HARD TO SAY GOODBYE

"Someday it may happen that a victim must be found who never will be missed." - W.S. Gilbert

He dropped Rocko off at his apartment, still unaware of Rocko's involvement to set him up, but he was fed up with Rocko's slip ups. He didn't want to kill him, so he decided from that moment forward he would cut off his life line to the streets.

While driving around listening to The Geto Boys song "Geto Boys and Girls," flash backs of the events that just transpired began to consume the space in his mind. He couldn't believe Blue's back stabbing ways and that Blue was actually trying to bring him a move. He remembered his mother once told him that true friends aren't supposed to cross you, but sometimes you gotta watch your friends closer than you have to watch your enemies because as soon as jealousy begins to eat at the core of their honor, the result can be compared to having full blown AIDS. It's no reversing it. "Fuck him!" He said to himself.

He was living on the dark side, and really didn't give a fuck about who he took there. It was either him or you, and he felt justified in whacking Blue.

Flash backs of Twitch and his dad getting gunned down right in front of him took over his mind and ignited his murderous appetite even more. Years had passed since their demise, but he still carried around a heavy heart for them. The face of the man responsible haunted him since he was 11, and he would never be able to completely rest until he was able to look that man in the eye and watch him take his last breath. His thoughts were interrupted from his pager vibrating in his pocket. It was Stacy.

Instead of calling, he drove to her house and blew the horn for her to come out. Stacy looked out of her bed room window and came outside.

"It's a good thing my father is sleep, cause he would've had a fit if he heard you blow the horn at 3 am in the morning."

"What you doing still up?" He asked.

"I couldn't sleep cause I haven't heard from you all day. What's going on D?"

"What do you mean what's going on? I been working all day painting houses and one of my co-workers was insubordinate, so he had to be dealt with accordingly."

"Well, I'm just glad you're safe. It's late, why don't you come in and spend the night and leave before noon when my father gets up."

The thought of lying in bed with Stacy was just the stress reliever he needed. He got in the shower and washed up. Scar woke up with an appetite for some cereal and came up from his room in the basement and heard the shower water running. He wondered what his daughter was doing up at 3 am taking a shower, but dismissed the thought as he sat down at the kitchen table and began to eat his cereal and read the paper. The shower cut off and his curiosity kicked in again. He looked up at the ceiling "Fuck is she doing up this time in the morning?!" Dontay was drying off when Scar got up from the table and walked to the bottom of the steps.

He looked up and began to tip toe up the steps when he heard foots steps walking down the hallway. As he made his way to the top of the steps, he saw the door to his daughter's bedroom close. "She must've had a bad dream or something and needed to take a shower he thought, as he made his way back to the kitchen. He dumped the rest of his cereal in the garbage disposal and went back to sleep.

Dontay got in bed with Stacy and made love to her until he fell asleep. Stacy laid there and while he slept, she thought of having a more substantive relationship with him. She knew he was involved in more than what he led her to believe, and she knew that he cared for her; but wondered if he would give her more of his time if he knew she was pregnant with his son. She wondered if he would ever love her the way she desired or if he was even capable of loving anyone else other than his self. She held back from telling him that she was having his baby because she was undecided if she would even keep it. She didn't want to be just another baby momma with no father for her son. She wanted stability, a family, a husband. She fell in love with him but was there enough room in his life, and any room in his heart for her and a child?

4 hours later at 7am the Sun had risen and day light had awakened him. Stacy was still asleep and he didn't want to wake her. He got up and got dressed. He leaned over a kissed her on her forehead then tip toed down the steps and let his self out. He went home and got in the shower to get ready for the day when his pager started vibrating. Kool was paging him with his code; how much money he had for him and the building address to meet him at "44-30-1723." He took a nap that lasted longer than he had planned. He got dressed and made his way to Montana Terrace at 9pm. He pulled up in the alley by the basketball court where Kool was leaning up against his car on his Motorola cell phone. Dontay got out of the car

and was caught by the mean mug stares from Marquise who was standing by the recreation center with a baseball bat in his hand.

"What's wrong with your man?" Dontay asked as he nodded his head in Marquise's direction.

"Don't pay that nigga no attention. Here you go playboy." He handed Dontay a paper bag with the 30 grand inside. "I'm almost done with that other thing, but shit been moving jive fast, so I'mma need you to push a few more of them thangs my way."

"I got you slim."

Dontay walked to the back of his car to put the money Kool gave him in the trunk. Marquise noticed a homeless man pushing the shopping cart from around the corner of the Rec. center. Staggering in his walk and appearing to be drunk, Marquise watched him closely as he crept up behind him.

As the homeless man edged closer and closer towards Dontay, Marquise noticed him reaching inside of his cart and pulled out a shot gun. The loud crack sound caused the birds in the trees and on the power lines to disperse and Kool and Dontay quickly looked from behind the trunk. Marquise was standing over top of him with the bat in his hand, and the homeless man laid face down on the ground with a gash in his head wide as the size of a ruler and his shot gun beside the shopping cart.

Marquise and Dontay locked eyes, and just gave each other a head nod.

"Who the fuck is this?" Dontay asked.

"I don't know, but this nigga was on your line." Marquise said as he picked up the shot gun.

Dontay walked over to the man laid out on the ground and kicked him over on his back. He removed his hoody and the sun shades he had on so he could see his face and stood there in a trance. "Help me tie this nigga up."

Dontay got the duct tape from out his trunk. He bounded his legs together at the ankles, and his hands behind him and tossed him in the back of his trunk.

As he drove off, he thought about how backwards life could be sometimes. The one person he never thought would cross him tried to bring him the ultimate move that would have took him off the count; and the one person that he thought wanted him off the count for his own selfish reasons, just saved his life.

He called the one nigga that he never had to second guess and told him to meet him at Langdon Park swimming pool. Within in minutes, C.C. pulled up and made his way through the hole in the fence to see Dontay swimming laps. Dontay came to the wall of the pool and climbed up on the ladder. He grabbed a towel and dried off.

"You ain't gonna believe what I got." He looked at C.C. and said. Nothing seemed out of the ordinary to C.C. because it was the norm for Dontay to go swimming at night when the pool was closed and sometimes call him to the pool for a meeting, but something seemed different this time. Dontay seemed excited as if he just hit a lick for 200 bricks and a millie. C.C. followed him to the shower room and in the back to the rest room, where he saw the bound and gagged body laying on the floor.

"Who the fuck is that?" C.C. curiously asked as he looked over at Dontay.

"This here is the mu'fucka I been looking for all my life." He said as he pulled the hoody off his head to reveal the large scar on the right side of his face.

"This is the mu'fucka that killed Twitch and my Dad." Dontay squatted down beside him and said "Damn homie! You a hard person to catch up with. I been lookin' forward to this day for 9 years. Do you remember me?" Scar remained quiet and stared at Dontay trying to place the face. He looked puzzled as to why he was asking if he remembered him. He only knew Dontay from the picture Redman gave him. He mumbled through the gag in his mouth. Dontay removed it to hear what he had to say. "I don't know you from nowhere. I was hired to stop your clock."

"Hired by who?"

"I can't tell you that."

Dontay stood up. "You can't tell me that huh?! You gonna tell me something." And on que he hit Scar in the mouth with the hardest punch he could possibly throw. Scar's head snapped back and hit the wall. That punch was followed up by a barrage of punches from C.C. Dontay wondered just how much this old timer was able to take before he started spitting out the name of who sent him. "O.K., O.K... I'll tell you! He exhaled... I'll tell you!" He said as he spit out blood and tried to gather his composure. Dontay grabbed C.C. by the arm to stop him from breaking Scar's entire face. He told Dontay that Detective Redman was the one who sent him because they were in his way and he couldn't sell his coke as long as Dontay and Rocko were around.

He told Dontay that nothing was personal, he was just doing his job and that the hit on his dad was because of the BLUE bag that was stole from his boss. Dontay stood there in a trance and thought for a second that it was the BLUE bags that he picked up the night Kool got hit by the car that his dad took to Hanover and had his runner sell for him.

"Get up!" Dontay grabbed Scar underneath his arm pit to help him up on his feet and walked him out towards the pool.

"Listen, I'm a business man and I understand how business goes more than anybody, but this business right here is personal. Putting a bullet in your head is too easy for you. I want you to know how it feels to know you're gonna die." He pushed Scar in the pool, and jumped in after him. He pulled him to the bottom of 12 feet, and looked him in his eyes as he struggled to hold his breath. He held him there until Scar's eyes began to bulge out of his face, and he couldn't hold his breath any longer. The look of knowing he was about to die in a matter of seconds was priceless. Since he was 11 years old he wanted to see the man responsible for killing his dad suffer. He continued to hold him there until Scar's body went stiff and the very last bubble exited his mouth. Dontay let him go and swam back to the top for air. Minutes later Scar's body rose to the top of the water and they left him there.

As they were leaving the pool, he turned to C.C. and told him to find out where Detective Redman lives, where his wife works, where his kids go to school and anything else he could find on this mu'fucka so they can pay him a visit since he wanna fuck around in these streets like he's a gangster. "We gonna show this mu'fucka how gangstaz play out here. Suit up big boi, we got one last house to paint."

CHAPTER
TWENTYSIX

GUILTY UNTIL PROVEN INNOCENT

"Government and luck are necessary in life, but only a fool trust either one of them."

-P.J. O'Rourke

Back at the homicide division, Detective Black sat at her desk going through her notes and researching the database for individuals that go by the nickname DB. She stared at the computer screen and rubbed her eyes, then looked down at her watch. Her partner walked over and offered her a cup of coffee. "No thanks. I had 2 cups already."

"Why don't you go home and get some rest. You been here working this case for the last 2 days around the clock."

"Yeah, maybe you're right." She stood up and grabbed her purse from the arm of her chair and listened as her colleagues in the office tell stories about some of the wildest arrest they made since being on the force. One officer told a story about how a suspect shitted on his self in the back seat of his car and began putting it all over him so they wouldn't touch him. "And believe me, we ain't touch his ass either."Said the officer as they all began to laugh.

Detective Black was gathering her things, and about to make her way towards the elevator when another officer told a story about how he had a guy in custody that was scared shitless to even mention this guy's name like he was the fuckin' grim reaper, and if he said his name he would drop dead right there where he stood. "I swear, I never seen a man so damn scared of this guy Dontay Beltre." Said the officer.

Detective Black spun around like a woman possessed. "Who did you say?!"

"Dontay Beltre?" The officer replied.

"Oh my fuckin' God! That's him! This son of a bitch. That's my suspect."

She silenced the entire office. The lieutenant approached her and asked her if she was sure and what proof did she have other than a popped necklace with his initials on it and a detective telling a story about him. "Don't jump the gun on this one detective. We have a fellow officer dead on this case. Regardless if he's been compromised or not, he was still one of us so make sure you're 100% right on this one before you make a move.

CHAPTER

TWENTYSEVEN

I CAN FEEL IT IN THE AIR

"True audacity is the trick of knowing how far you can go, in going too far." –SB

After taking care of Scar, he set his sights on the crooked cop that was responsible for orchestrating the killings of Twitch and his dad over the *Blue Bags* of cocaine. They strapped up with their Mac-11 submachine guns that could easily be concealed under their jackets, and got on their Suzuki RM-Z250 dirt bikes for a quick and easy get away out to the location that his contact at the DMV gave him of Detective Ronald Redman's place of residence. He didn't know what to expect when him and C.C. pulled up, but was ready to deal with any and everything that got in his way of putting an end to the man that was partly responsible for his Dad's murder. They turned their bikes off and sat there for a minute watching the house. This was a different kind of mission from when they waited for Pierre. He wasn't so easily removed from the mission until it was done. He refused to let anger cloud his intellect and rush him into making a hasty decision. Every move and every step had to be thought out carefully, and he was willing to wait as long as it took. He surveyed every inch of the house and noticed that there was a 6 foot wooden fence between the house and the garage was slightly ajar. "Come on!" He told C.C. as he took off his helmet, put his hoody over his head and walked over to the fence. Once inside the backyard area, he noticed the bare, dry earth landscape was littered with lumber scarps, stacks of concrete cinder blocks, tangled loops of wire, and PVC pipes discarded by the roofers working on the house. He peeped back through the gaps in the wooden fence and had a clear view to the street. There, they could easily see when Redman pulled up in his car. "Here he come! As soon as he gets out the car, his ass is mines!" Dontay anxiously said as he tightly clutched his Mac 11.

Detective Redman instantly noticed the two unfamiliar dirt bikes parked on the opposite side of the street when he pulled up. His cop instincts kicked in and he rolled down his windows and sat there for a moment, listening for any strange sounds. Nothing but silence came to him, but something still didn't sit well with him about the strange bikes parked across the street from his house. He pulled off surveying the area until he turned the corner at the end of his street where he pulled over, turned off his headlights, put on his night vision binoculars and watched his street for any strange trespassers.

"Shit! He left! Come on, let's see if we can catch up with him Dontay said as he led the way back to their bikes.

Detective Redman rose up in his seat once he saw the two men emerge from the darkness of his backyard and got into the car. He started his car and the roar from the engine and his headlights sent a warning signal to Dontay. He looked up the street and saw Detective Redman's car speeding towards them. He pulled out his Mack 11 and began unloading a barrage of bullets before detective Redman could react. He ducked down behind the steering wheel and put the car in reverse. Dontay and C.C. jumped on their bikes and gave chase. Detective Redman weaved in and out of traffic as fast as he could, but Dontay and C.C. were hot on his tail. He ran every stop sign and every red light in an attempt to lose his would be attackers nearly hitting pedestrians standing at the curve.

Dontay didn't want to waste any more bullets, so he waited for Redman to make his first mistake. C.C. got close to Detective Redman's car on the passenger's side and raised his gun, but before he could get a good enough aim, Redman swerved his car in an attempt to try and knock C.C. into a parked car. He almost lost control, but was swift with his handle of the bike and swerved out of the way of the parked car and rode onto the sidewalk. His Mack

11 dangled from a strap around his neck as he regained control of his bike.

Dontay got close enough to fire off a few more shots, but hit nothing but air.

Detective Redman made a quick turn onto the beltway and mashed on the gas. C.C. rode up on his passenger's side and fired off rapid shots causing Detective Redman to lower his head as he continued to make his getaway. His entire career has been full of danger and tragedy. He always calmly confronted danger at its worst head on, but something peculiar was happening. He was starting to panic. Fear had pried into him, touching a deep and primitive level where nothing else had ever reached him before. He broke out into a cold sweat, and had no clue as to who is pursuers were. He kept his eyes straight forward out of fear that he would crash, but his panic began to swell, and as the more gunshots hit his car; the more he felt that he was in grave peril. Rapid gun shots continued to rip through the threads of his car. A single shot pierced his left shoulder from Dontay's gun which caused him to swerve into the concrete barrier. He tried to regain control when another bullet hit him in the neck. Still not ready to accept his fate, Detective Redman put his hand over his neck and stepped on the gas. He saw his only way of survival a thousand yards ahead of him. The flashing lights of a state trooper had pulled over on the shoulder ahead. Dontay saw the flashing lights but also saw the exit. He sped up to get closer to

Detective Redman's car, aimed his gun at Detective Redman's head and shot at the driver's side window and turned off on the exit. Detective Redman never slowed down, at a hundred miles per hour; barely missed the state trooper's squad car and crashed into the woods.

Dontay and C.C. made their getaway back to the city without any problems. They parked their bikes in C.C.'s garage, got rid of their guns, and went their separate ways.

Dontay made it home and called Stacy to come keep him company, then took a nice hot shower feeling on top of the world after his long awaited opportunity to put an end to the men responsible for his Dad's murder. He went to the basement and looked at some old home movies and reminisced of their times together. Suddenly, he was interrupted by continuous loud knocking at his front door.

He jumped up and ran up the steps with his gun in hand, locked and loaded.

"F.B.I.!!!!" OPEN UP BEFORE WE KICK IT DOWN!" Were the strong words that came through the door from the deep voiced heavy set white man that stood on the other side with what looked like the entire squad from Montgomery County Emergency Response Team, Local and Federal Task Force, operation Safe Streets, DC Homicide, ATF and DEA all dressed in their black tactical gear, black helmets with gas masks on their faces and armed with their M4 assault rifles. The alphabet boys were in full effect and Dontay had one of two options. Either leave in their custody dead or alive.

"WE GOT THE HOUSE SURROUNDED! COME OUT WITH YOUR HANDS UP!"

"Shit!" He said as he took off running to the third level of the house and hide his gun in the stash spot he had built into the floor of the attic, and without further warning, they kicked the door off the hinges and stormed the house like a stampede of raging bulls.

"F.B.I.! GET DOWN ON THE FUCKIN' GROUND NOW!"

He surrendered without a struggle, and figured since he was sitting on some paper that could buy the best defense team in the city, he could beat whatever they charged him with.

Moreover, as long as C.C. was still on the streets, no witness would dare come to court.

CHAPTER

TWENTYEIGHT

IF IT AIN'T ROUGH, IT AIN'T RIGHT

WE NEVER TRAVELED DOWN THE ROAD OF LEAST RESISTANCE. -SB

Stacy pulled up to what looked like every police car in the DMV only to see the man she thought of building a life with in handcuffs. She couldn't believe her eyes. **"What could he have possibly done that called for all this?!** She wondered as she looked on in despair. She rubbed on her stomach and then looked down at it. She was 7 months pregnant with his son and couldn't imagine raising a boy alone without his dad.

Memories of everything she saw started to replay in her mind. The pictures of him the detective gave her dad, the bags she saw him take into the house after their trip from Vegas; were all starting to paint a clearer picture of him being involved in more than what he led her to believe. She made a U-turn and went on her way totally unaware that she would be going home to bad news about her own dad.

Shortly after Stacy had pulled off, Dontay was transported

to the local police station in Montgomery County, where he saw the Magistrate Judge to waive extradition. 48 hours later he was in DC Central Cell getting finger printed and booked for multiple homicides. Everything that his teachers told him about mixing MONEY and MURDER will bring a world of MAYHEM became as clear as day to him.

A few weeks had passed since his arrest, and he was being bussed from the DC Jail to DC District Court in the U.S. Marshalls van along with one other prisoner with similar charges. Dontay remained silent and kept his eyes glued to the streets watching the passing cars as they rode down Pennsylvania Avenue. He fiddled around with the handcuff key he had hidden underneath his tongue, waiting for the right opportunity to un-cuff his self.

The van pulled into the underground garage and came to a stop at the entry elevator that led to the holding area where he waited to speak with his attorney. The cases his attorney dropped on him were weak. All of the circumstantial evidence they had, he didn't see it sticking. However, he was suspected of 1 cop killing and things would get crazy in the prosecutor's office if they charged him with that case.

"We have another problem." His attorney said as he opened his briefcase and pulled out the

Washington Post newspaper and dropped it on the table in front of him. Dontay stared down at the photo on the front page and couldn't believe his eyes when he saw his self with the caption that read "The Teflon Suspect!"

"This is bad." He said as he looked at his attorney "What can we do?"

"Well for starters, we're gonna ask that the case be dismissed, and if he doesn't budge on that,

we're gonna ask for a change of venue, because any jury will be prejudice and bias towards you in DC after reading this and a conviction will be inevitable. We can't put up a defense against this article, but we damn sure gonna try."

"I don't need you to try, I need you to pull some strings and get this pushed back as far as you can so it won't be so fresh in their mind."

"I'll see what I can do."

His attorney got up and exited the holding area. Dontay sat and waited to be arraigned and the stress was building. His case was called and he was escorted into the court room.

Stacy was front and center amongst the spectators and the look on her face didn't reveal a look of pleasure to see him. He smiled at her, and blew a kiss her way that was reciprocated with a cold stare and mean mugs.

The judge entered the courtroom and the proceedings began. He was firm in his stance and didn't think twice about denying the motion for dismissal, the motion for a change of venue and every other motion the defense presented.

"This man is in front of me with multiple homicides and dubbed "The Teflon Suspect" by the Washington Post. Only two other men in American history have been labeled with such a strong description of their character… John Gotti, who was called "The Teflon Don" because of his numerous acquittals for murder, and Ronald Reagan who was labeled "The Teflon President" when he was faced with the crisis in 1986-87 and accused of having knowledge of weapon sells through Israeli brokers to Iran in exchange for the release of U.S. hostages being held in Lebanon. So Mr. Beltre is obviously by some standards, a dangerous individual, and you can't possibly expect me to release him just because he appeared in the newspaper. That isn't how this works Mr. Moore. I wanna see more evidence before I make any ruling or consider any motions. Clear your calendars gentlemen, I'm setting a preliminary hearing for September 9th." The judge slammed his gavel down hard and exited the courtroom. The tone was set for what to expect from this judge, and Mr. Moore was already trying to figure out how to get the case moved to another judge's docket. "You gotta have confidence in your ability to win. We're not gonna give this diabolical mu'fucka the pleasure of saying we ran from him. He's only the judge. It's the evidence that makes the case, and Imma make sure that there isn't any."

Dontay tried to boost confidence into his attorney, then looked back at the crowd of spectators and saw Stacy put on her shades, stood up out of her seat, and left the courtroom without anything as much as a wave bye. He noticed the bulge in her stomach, and stared at her until she was completely out of sight. "She couldn't be." He said to himself as the marshal escorted him back to the holding area.

They put him in a cell with a small bench that was being occupied by someone who was apparently trying to get some rest. He sat up on the bench when he heard the loud clank sound of the steel gate open, and moved over to allow Dontay to sit down.

"Thanks slim, I appreciate it."

"No problem homes."

Dontay noticed the guy's attire and asked him if he just got locked up.

"Naw, I just got sentenced. Mu'fuckaz gave me 25 to life, but the first chance I get, I'm outta here."

Dontay fiddled around with the handcuff key in his mouth and shared the same thoughts.

"LET'S GO!" The marshal ordered as he unlocked the steel gate and handcuffed and shackled them together.

"What's your name?" Dontay asked as they walked down the long hallway towards the elevator.

"Big Mike."

"O.K. Big Mike, I'm D. Check this out." Dontay flashed the handcuff key in his mouth. "When we get in the van, we gonna go to the back and the first chance I get, Imma take the cuffs and shackles off, and when they open the door; we gonna make our move. You wit it?"

"Damn right, I'm wit it! I'm not trying to do 25 to life up in this joint."

They got into the van and went to the back seats as planned. They exited the underground garage of the court building on to C. Street N.W. and headed towards the 3rd street tunnel, when a speeding black Mazda 929 swerved in front of the van causing the driver to lose control and side swipe the wall of the tunnel in an attempt to avoid a collision. He tried to regain control and gave the steering wheel a hard pull to the right, hitting the car in the opposite lane. He stepped on the brake several times, but to no avail the van wouldn't stop. The driver weaved in and out of traffic trying to avoid every car in it's path when the Mazda cut him off once again, pushing the van over and causing him to side swipe the wall trying to avoid an accident.

Dontay and Big Mike struggled to stay in their seats as the van swerved side to side. Dontay tried to get the key out of his mouth when the van came in contact with the wall causing him to drop the key on the floor board of the van… **"Shit!"** He said as he tried to stick his foot out to retrieve the key, but the more the van swerved; the key impelled further and further out of his reach.

"What happened? Big Mike asked.

"I lost the key. It fell on the floor and I can't reach it."Ahhhh! Dontay said as he tried with all his might to stretch out his foot as far as he could. The van finally came to a stop when it crashed into the concrete causing everyone to jerk forward then back against their seat fast and hard. Smoke began to seep from under the hood and the smell of gas began to fill Big Mike's nostrils "You smell that? He asked, but received no response. He looked at the driver who was unresponsive, then over at Dontay who was knocked out from the impact of the crash. Big Mike stretched his body as far as the handcuffs and shackles would allow him in an attempt to retrieve the handcuff key from under the seat. He noticed flames coming from under the hood as he was now in a race against time. The flames were starting to grow larger and larger. A hundred yards ahead, the driver of the Mazda exited the vehicle and walked towards the crash. Smoke began to fill the inside of the van and caused Big Mike to cover his mouth, but was still choking from the smoke slowly but surely entering his lungs. Big Mike was able to get the handcuff key and unlock his self. In a frantic panic, he slapped and shook Dontay in an attempt to wake him up. Dontay was groggy, but coming to as flames were now coming through the dash board of the van. Big Mike began to kick the windows as hard as he could in an attempt to free his self, but the steel screen covers that were placed over the windows for security reasons were making it virtually impossible to get through. Dontay was semi unconscious and thoughts began to fill his head. Voices were muffled around him and his vision was blurry. He thought of Stacy and how he would never get a chance to see her again. The smoke grew thicker and the flames made their way to the front seat and were inching their way through the entire vehicle. The van was now engulfed in flames, and thoughts of all of his nefarious ways, and all the wrong he did in his life, allowed him to be ready to accept Allah's punishment of being burnt alive. The back door of the van flung open and Big Mike shot outta there like a 223 from an AK-47. Dontay closed his eyes and was on the verge of fainting when a tug at his shoulders pulled him inch by inch over the back seat. Flames were now at the tip of his feet as he was being pulled more and more over the seat, and without warning; the van exploded into a ball of flames filling the air with a thick cloud of black smoke.

"It is Allah that takes the souls of men at death, and those that die not; he takes during their sleep. Those on whom he has passed the decree of death, he keeps back from returning to life, but the rest he sends to their bodies for a term appointed. Certainly in this are signs for those who reflect." –The Holy Quran 39:41

TO BE CONTINUED...

EPILOGUE

To all the men and women I forgot to mention in my acknowledgement: In no way, form or fashion did I forget about you, it's too many to name. Keep your heads up homies and remember that strength grows out of adversity. Our struggle toughens the human spirit. Most people try to travel the road of least resistance, but we always grabbed the bull by the horns and faced the roughness of every situation head on. Most people don't understand us, our way of life, our culture, the code of honor that we live & die to protect. They don't understand how we're able to walk these basketball score type of sentences with our heads held high, with our physical and mental health still intact and our minds sharp as a knife.

Nothing in life worth having is ever achieved without a struggle. Keep fighting for your freedom, and keep fighting to survive, and Never Give Up! My strongest salute to you all. Much Love & Respect.

SEAN BRANCH

Sean Branch, best known as "Teflon Sean" is a thriving entrepreneur from Washington DC. He's the founder and CEO of T.E.F.L.O.N. Sports Apparel with a degree in business from Pueblo Community College. Recently released from prison after serving 25 years for a crime he did not commit, he held true to form to the "no snitch" code of the streets. While incarcerated, he was compelled to write about a period in DC history when making fast money was the order of the day and the violence and chaos that came along with it was commonplace. Sean hopes to inspire others that have dealt with similar situations to utilize their skills to maximize their potential financially.

CPSIA information can be obtained
at www.ICGtesting.com
Printed in the USA
LVHW031627091219
639927LV00013B/919/P